A THEORY OF LOVE

A THEORY OF LOVE

A NOVEL

MARGARET BRADHAM THORNTON

ecco

An Imprint of HarperCollins*Publishers*

 For information address HarperCollins Publishers, 195 Broadway, New York, NY 10007.

HarperCollins books may be purchased for educational, business, or sales promotional use. For information please e-mail the Special Markets Department at SPsales@harpercollins.com.

FIRST EDITION

Designed by Michelle Crowe
Title page images by Robyn Mackenzie/Shutterstock, Inc.

Library of Congress Cataloging-in-Publication Data has been applied for.

ISBN 978-0-06-274270-4

18 19 20 21 22 LSC 10 9 8 7 6 5 4 3 2 1

The World was all before them, where to choose
Thir place of rest, and Providence thir guide:
They hand in hand with wandring steps and slow,
Through Eden took thir solitarie way.

—*Paradise Lost*

A THEORY OF LOVE

CHAPTER ONE

BERMEJA

Twice the pilot dipped low and waved a wing to a fisherman who waved back. Christopher shifted his surfboard and stood it beside him. He watched the small plane disappear down the coast. He looked back at the fishing boats and sea that glistened as if cut from translucent stone. He remembered a retired sea captain telling him that he would always know where he was by the color of the sea. He said he could be blindfolded and dropped in any body of water and the moment he took off his blindfold, he would know where he was. The idea of color as a type of compass—a form of geography—had enthralled Christopher. The captain had been the caretaker of the land that now surrounded him.

He heard the hum of tires on the river-stone road before he saw them—the hotel manager with a young woman in the passenger seat. They stopped to see if he wanted a ride. He had noticed her yesterday getting out of a taxi at the entrance to the small hotel. She was dressed in an ankle-length skirt and wore a fedora. Since his arrival in Bermeja two weeks ago, Christopher had watched crews from L.A. come and go—one for a photo shoot for an expensive brand of suntan oils, another for a bathing suit ad. There was something about her that made him know she was not from the West Coast.

He angled his surfboard into the back and got in. "You look as if you're going to give a lecture," he said, leaning forward, looking at her blazer and the satchel she held on her lap.

She shook her head and smiled. "I'm going to interview Paolo Pavesi." Helen referred to the eccentric Italian financier who had spent the last two decades transforming Bermeja into a glamorous bohemian refuge.

He nodded and asked her how long she was staying.

"I'm leaving day after tomorrow."

Christopher asked the hotel manager to drop him off at Playa Azul, the small beach cupped between high cliffs a quarter of a mile south of the hotel. Helen watched as he took his surfboard from the back of the jeep. She could tell by the way he handled it, it was a familiar object. But if he had once been a surfer, he didn't appear to be one now. He was lean and tanned, but his skin had not been punished by years and years in the sun.

He noticed her watching him. As he thanked the hotel manager, he hung his free hand on the roll bar and leaned in toward her. "So, should we have dinner tonight at eight or nine?"

She laughed and brushed the hair from her face.

Helen had not shown up for dinner, but the following morning Christopher walked down to the hotel and caught her getting coffee.

"You didn't show up last night. I waited at the bar for hours."

"I'm not so sure you did."

He mimed being stabbed in the chest.

"I didn't think it was a real invitation. I don't even know your name."

"Christopher Delavaux. And it was. How about tonight?"

"I can't. I've been invited to a dinner party at Mr. Pavesi's. At Casa de Mi Corazón."

He raised his eyebrows. "You might want to be careful."

"Why?"

"Well, it can get pretty decadent around here." He paused. "Or so I'm told."

"Really?" She waited for an explanation.

"When you met with Paolo, how many young women were sunbathing nude? I'm guessing three or four."

"Four."

"Did he give you a tour of his house?"

"He did."

"Did he show you his studio?"

"You mean the room with the mats on the floor and the slits and small round openings in the domed ceiling?"

He tilted his head. "Well then, I rest my case. So if you bring me along, I'll look after you."

She bit her lower lip and thought for a minute. "Okay. Yeah, okay."

"Meet you here at nine."

"How do you know the time?"

"I was invited, too."

He started to leave but hesitated. "I can count on you to show up this time?"

"Don't you need to know my name?"

He smiled and shook his head.

CHAPTER TWO

BERMEJA

Bermeja was the name given to the eight-mile stretch along Mexico's Pacific coast halfway between Puerto Vallarta and Acapulco. Surrounded by a thirty-six-thousand-acre nature preserve, Bermeja was referred to as the land where nobody was born and nobody died. Protected by high cliffs and jungles and wetlands, it was often separated on its eastern boundary by flooding rivers. It was land that was so useless for agriculture that no roads existed before the 1960s. A Venezuelan family a century earlier had acquired the stretch of coastline as part of a complicated land deal. The third wife of Christopher's grandfather had inherited much of the land, but when she died young without any heirs, her family reclaimed it. They had little use for the small house on top of a high cliff, so they granted their deceased daughter's husband a ninety-nine-year lease.

The next generation of the same Venezuelan family sold all the surrounding land along with the lease to Paolo Pavesi, who, it was rumored, had fled Milan over irregularities in the accounts of his family's privately held bank. Whether he had to choose between going to jail or leaving Italy or whether it had been love at first sight or an unanswerable obsession, there was no question for him but to head west. With the ease of a chameleon, he anointed himself protector of the land and professed himself to be a picture framer on the grandest scale. After he had purchased the land of Bermeja, Pavesi stayed in the house granted by lease to Christopher's grandfather as he and his architect made plans for others. A small number of houses were built into the sides of cliffs, with open-air *palapas,* curved stucco walls painted in bright saffrons, hot pinks, and ultramarine blues, and pools that did not interrupt the line of the Pacific. Over time a trickle of Europeans—the son of a famous artist, an heir to an industrial conglomerate, a rock star, a retired businessman turned philosopher-poet—followed and built their own houses.

In appreciation for the loan of the house, Pavesi added a large *palapa* and pool to the Delavaux property. He christened it Casa Tortuga because, in the year of his arrival, sea turtles began nesting on the beaches and had continued each year since. No one could explain this change in the nesting habits of the turtles, but Pavesi took it as a sign that nature approved of what he was doing.

At nine o'clock, Helen was in the hotel lobby with the photographer who had been assigned to work with her. He had just arrived when Christopher pulled up in an open-topped jeep.

"Helen," he called. "Ready?"

"How do you know my name?" she asked as she climbed in.

"Bermeja is a small place," he said. He pointed to lights at the top of the northernmost cliff. "See those lights? That's where I'm staying—Casa Tortuga. Alfonso looks after it, and since I arrived two weeks ago, he's been beside himself that I do nothing except read and surf and go for runs by myself. When you appeared alone—well, word traveled quickly."

She paused, recalibrating her assumptions. "So why are you here?" she asked.

He explained that he was taking a month off between working for a New York law firm and starting an investment firm with one of his clients. "My mother used to bring us here. We stayed in the same place—Casa Tortuga—but it was much simpler back then." He pointed back to the top of the cliff.

"Us?"

"My sister, Laure, and me."

She asked him if his parents were divorced. He explained that, when he was thirteen, his father and his father's best friend were killed in a skiing accident. "They were excellent skiers, but they took risks they shouldn't have. They were skiing off-piste and got caught in an avalanche. My mother wasn't far away when it happened. After that she could never look at the color white without hearing the loud hissing of that avalanche. I think she started bringing Laure and me here because of the colors and because there weren't any memories." Christopher ran past words as if running past darkness.

"We came here for years. It was the only place my mother didn't seem sad. Back then it was all wilderness—no other houses except the shack near the beach where the caretaker lived. Laure and I would spend all our time with him. He would saddle up these wild renegade ponies and take us riding on the beaches, and we would disappear all day exploring in the jungle. If we got thirsty, he would slice open a coconut; if we got hungry, he would give us the meat of a prickly pear wrapped in a tortilla. My mother sometimes even came with us. She lived a very formal existence, but here—for a brief period each year—everything changed. This is the first time I've been back here since then." He seemed to be talking to himself, as if he were working out something he needed to understand. He had never told someone so much about himself so quickly.

Ahead the road forked. He shifted down a gear. "I think it's this one." He took the left turn and they climbed higher. "So tell me again, what brings you here?"

"I'm here to write an article on Bermeja."

"For?"

"The London *Sunday Times*."

"You live in London?"

"I do."

"Interesting."

"Because?"

"I'm moving to London."

"Seriously?" She pushed back sideways to look at him. She was not certain he was telling the truth.

"It's where we're locating our business."

"Why?"

"Oh, you know, halfway between the U.S. and China, most European cities are an hour or two away." He stopped in front of gateposts made from tree trunks. Beyond was a pathway lit by candles in large glass cylinders.

"I think this is the entrance. Look familiar?"

"Yes, but it's hard to tell at night."

"Did Paolo show you the hanging bridge?" Christopher referred to the rope bridge that hung from the top of the cliff where Pavesi's house was located to the equally high, rocky island some three hundred feet away.

"He did, but we didn't go on it. It looked dodgy. It was windy and it was swaying back and forth."

"You should have. The island is extraordinary—like one of those tepuis in South America except this one is covered in wild tropical trees. If it hadn't been so difficult to get to, Paolo would have built his house there."

As they turned in to the entrance, a man they presumed to be the majordomo approached and spoke to Christopher in Spanish. Christopher thanked him and backed up to change directions.

"The dinner party's been switched to Playa Azul," he said, lifting his chin in the direction of the man with whom he had just been speaking. "He said a large group from Madrid who are staying down the coast were added at the last moment. So Paolo moved the party to the beach."

"Where is Playa Azul?"

"It's the beach where you dropped me off yesterday—south of the hotel."

He drove even more slowly down the twisting road, testing his brakes before each curve, listening for cars.

"So is it true what they say about Mr. Pavesi?"

"About his being involved in financial scandal and fleeing Italy to avoid jail? Who knows. I've never looked into it. This is the first time I've met him. But you know, sometimes when someone does something remarkable, especially if it's unusual, people like to find explanations that diminish the achievement—often with tinges of impropriety. Maybe it's an oblique form of jealousy. When I first came here over twenty-five years ago, there was nothing—no electricity, barely any roads. It was rough. When I heard he had bought all this land, I assumed it would be destroyed by development, but just the opposite has happened. He's been a wonderful protector—he's created his own version of Sacro Bosco. If this place had fallen into the wrong hands, it would have been destroyed. So I find it hard to believe that someone who loves this place, loves beauty as much as Paolo does, could be all bad."

Helen noticed that Christopher had a way of letting a sentence slide to a stop to indicate the end of the discussion.

"Are all the interiors of the houses painted the same as Mr. Pavesi's?"

"Every one that I've seen. Of the thirteen houses, I've been in—I don't know—maybe five or six. Paolo decided that only colors found in the landscape could be used. That's why everything seems so harmonious. The interiors are designed to be as continuous as possible with the natural world. The blue of the ocean, the pink of the bougainvillea, the yellow of the sun—are all brought inside. He designed the houses never to lose contact with the sun or the ocean breezes or the night sky. That's why no house has paned windows, just openings. He and his architect spent months on-site recording the way the winds blow, where the sun sets, where the constellations in the night sky appear, before deciding exactly where to position each house. That's why in every room, there's always a breeze and no opening gets too much sun. Paolo deserves all the credit for this place—there are no big boats or landing strips for private jets. It mainly attracts rich artists and wealthy Europeans who want a break from people." He pulled close to the side of the road to let an approaching car pass. "So how's the article coming?"

"Good. I think I'm getting what I need."

"Did Paolo show you the shrine to the sun?"

"The shrine to the sun?"

"The big concrete bowl that sits on the southern promontory at the end of his property. I'm surprised he didn't show it to you. Definitely worth mentioning in any article you're writing. It's not that far—maybe a twenty-minute drive away. Do you write for the travel section?"

"On occasion, like this one, but most of the time for the features section."

"Do you get to choose your subject?"

"Sometimes my editor suggests something, sometimes I come up with ideas."

"So what was your last article?"

"It was very short, just a column. The one before was on new trends in organic gardening, the one before that was—"

"What was the short one on?"

"Words."

"Words?"

"Yes, words that don't have counterparts in other languages—such as *schadenfreude* or *enamoramiento* or *shi.* It takes at least seven words in English to describe the emotion that the Germans can describe in one. English does not have a correct word for *enamoramiento*—it's translated in English as an infatuation or obsessive love but neither one is quite right. *Shi* means waiting to do something at the right time. It's the moment when everything is in harmony. Someone can wait all his or her life and never experience it. Chinese is the only language that has a word for it."

"So do you have a favorite word?"

"I do."

He ducked his chin and waited.

"*Neverness.*"

"*Neverness?*" He rolled the word as if he were trying to find something underneath it. "Is it a word?"

"Yes, invented by an English bishop in the seventeenth century. He wrote a dictionary of philosophical language, and he listed *neverness* underneath his entry for *everness,* which he defined as 'eternity, for ever and ever, always.' He left the definition for *neverness* blank. There's no word like it in English or any other language. There is *nothingness.* Keats used it in a sonnet."

"Spanish has *nadería.*"

"Similar but not the same."

"*Neverness.*" Christopher said the word as if it were breakable and he were putting it down on a hard surface. "It's rather hopeless—the opposite of infinity—incredibly sad, don't you think? Not sure I like it."

The road turned and descended toward the coast. Ahead they could see the sparkle of lanterns hung from trees.

"Here we are," he said and parked next to a few other small open-topped jeeps. "You might want to leave your sandals."

"So how about you, do you have a favorite word?"

"Favorite? Maybe not favorite, but one I like. *Sprezzatura*. Do you know it?"

She shook her head.

"'Studied nonchalance.' I don't think it has a one-word counterpart in any other language either. Could've been a word for you. I had an Italian teacher who required all of us to memorize the passage in Castiglione's *Book of the Courtier* where he says he has found a universal rule—I still remember it—'to avoid affectation in every way possible as though it were a rough and dangerous reef and to practice in all things a certain *sprezzatura* so as to make whatever one does look as if it is without effort or thought.' He thought the idea sublime—it was his goal to teach us all *sprezzatura*."

"And did he?"

He shrugged his shoulder and laughed, "I'm counting on you to tell me that."

They walked out to the beach. A table for forty had been set up with torches around the perimeter. As they approached, a server handed them margaritas with coral hibiscuses floating on top. Paolo Pavesi was in a full-length caftan, and on each arm hung one of the young women Helen had seen sunbathing around his pool earlier in the day. They were wearing matching long white halter dresses with small beads and shells embroidered around a deep V neckline. Paolo embraced Christopher and kissed Helen on both cheeks and brought them over to a group that included his son and daughter-in-law, a stylist and photographer on a fashion shoot for French *Vogue,* and two men who had come over from Mexico City to play polo. Everyone was polite but indifferent. When Christopher and Helen were included in the circle, the conversation continued in French.

He pulled her back and away from the group. They walked down to the edge of the water.

"So how is your French?"

"Rusty. I'm much better at listening than speaking."

"Spanish?"

"Nonexistent."

Paolo's son, Philippe, approached and asked Helen if she were getting everything she needed. He turned to Christopher and explained that he worked for Credit Suisse in Geneva. He had been in Los Angeles for a business meeting and had come down to Bermeja for a long weekend to see his father. As he and Christopher began to chat about the private equity market in Europe, Paolo clapped his hands and asked them all to find their places and enjoy the ceviche. He insisted that Helen sit next to him. Christopher found a place across from her, and he watched her as the conversation switched, by whim, from Italian to French to Spanish and then back to French. She had taken enough French in school to understand the French portion of the conversation, but she only caught shadows of what was being said in the other two languages. The group from down the coast did not arrive until ten thirty, when the main course of grilled fish was being served. A watermelon granita followed, and then Paolo stood up and raised his glass.

"Bermeja—is infused with the mysteries of life. We come here to discover for ourselves. And for us, like the returning sea turtles, we will all come back because the desire is so strong. With all this vastness"—he gestured to the ocean—"to remember so precisely, to know where they belong, to know where to come. And when we are here, we see with one eye and we feel with the other. It is here that we are our most creative selves. And after this wonderful dinner offered to us from the bounty of Bermeja, you are all invited to come with me to Casa de Mi Corazón. *Salut*!"

Christopher smiled at Helen and winked. Dinner disbanded, and Christopher joined her to thank Paolo for including them. Philippe caught Christopher before he disappeared. They agreed to meet in London.

As they walked back to the jeep, Christopher asked Helen, "So on a scale of one to ten, how insufferable?"

"It was okay. It would have been helpful if I had spoken two or three more languages."

"Yeah, well, I think Paolo does it on purpose. The first week I was here, I received an invitation to dinner, and during dinner he stood up and recited the thirty-three rules for ownership in Bermeja. I think he was making them up as he went along, but one of the rules was you had to speak at least three languages. Walking across the hanging bridge was another."

"He's just being anti-American or anti-English or both."

"You're probably right."

"I didn't follow what they were saying about the ceremony of the sun."

"I only heard a bit, but I think he was referring to the summer solstice. His giant bowl, or 'inverted temple,' as he sometimes calls it, is positioned in such a way on the southern promontory that at the end of the longest day of the summer, the sun descends into it."

"Oh, the shrine to the sun you mentioned."

He nodded. "I wasn't sure if you wanted to go to his house. Might have counted for interesting material for your article."

"My article's for the travel section. To inform readers about interesting places they might consider traveling to, not describing eccentrics with dark sides. So what do you think happens back at his house?"

"I don't know, but I can guess. More wine, some hashish, and then a slow free-for-all in his studio."

"Really?" She didn't know if he were telling the truth or teasing her.

“Only a guess.”

She understood he was doing both. “I did like what he said about the turtles returning, but his attempt to be a poet-philosopher—”

“Was a little weak. But still, ‘With all this vastness’ ”—Christopher gestured to the ocean with his chin—“ ‘to remember so precisely, to know where they belong, to know where to come.’ ”

She laughed. “Well, I liked what he said about one eye seeing and the other feeling.”

They arrived at the hotel and he turned to park.

“I can get out here.”

“So what are you up to tomorrow?”

“I’m going to spend the morning with Ben—the photographer I was meeting with when you picked me up—we need to go over all the shots, and then I leave for the airport at two.”

He nodded. “If you have time, come by Casa Tortuga. I’ll show you around. It’s worth seeing.” He leaned over and kissed her good night. “Bye, Helen.”

The next day, Helen kept hoping she would run into Christopher as she and Ben crisscrossed the land to different locations. At twenty past two, she finally closed the door of the taxi to head to the Manzanillo airport, but she told the driver she needed to make one stop. When she arrived at Casa Tortuga, she knocked on the front gate and called hello, but no one answered. She pushed the gate open. A passageway densely bordered with banana trees and periwinkle-blue plumbago led to a *palapa* overlooking the ocean. The view stunned her. She felt as if she could see the entire world from where she stood. But its vastness disoriented her and made her feel as if she could be swallowed without hesitation or notice.

To her left was the small house Christopher had described. She called again, but again, no one answered. A long narrow pool stretched along the contour of the cliff and formed a spine to the house. She crossed the space under the *palapa* and knocked on the open door. She called again and walked inside. It was simple—as if a cocoon offering protection. She understood how he could plan to stay for a month. She was reminded of Paolo Pavesi's words about returns. A pair of faded jeans, the ones Christopher had worn the night before, hung neatly over the back of a chair. On the bed a book on European economic history lay open facedown. Why had he told her to come by if he wasn't going to be here? She pulled a card from her bag, but she couldn't think of anything to say, so she just wrote her number and closed the book with her card marking its place.

CHAPTER THREE

BERMEJA

The morning air was soft and fresh and there was not even a whisper of a cloud in the sky. "Oh, God, not another fucking beautiful day." Christopher looked out over the ocean and quoted the line from *White Mischief* that had become the sarcastic mantra at his boarding school during his first year, when the rainy days of December darkness settled down at three thirty every afternoon. Even though it had been almost a quarter of a century ago, he knew that if you said something enough times it became like a tattoo you could never get rid of.

He was spending the entire month of January in Bermeja. He had come with no computer, no cell phone, a few books, but he mainly came back to look at the ocean and to be left alone. He had wanted to test for himself how it felt to return—as if he were daring himself to feel footprints again, to remember the color of the sea. Memories were always rearranging themselves like flocks of birds that shifted formation and changed altitude according to some unknown algorithm. In the *New York Times* he had read about a study of the diminutive brown creeper that kept flying into buildings in downtown Chicago. One that had been stunned, tagged, and released was found dead a block from where it had been found the year before. He wondered if memory and distance were some long-forgotten form of human migration.

He decided to drive down the coast to check out the waves the Spanish group had described as translucent tunnels running the length of the beach. He did not expect Helen to drop by. Girls like Helen never made an effort. If anything, they had learned never to grant a flirtatious comment, learned never to acknowledge how their bodies served as magnets when they walked across a crowded room, learned never to make the first move. He would not allow himself to think much about her. She would be a hard one to get to know, and he wasn't sure he wanted to make the effort.

As he drove south, he reminded himself that had he really wanted to see her again, he would either have never left to go surfing or would have told her to come to the beach where he would be—but he hadn't—so that had to indicate something. He stopped wondering about her when he saw the waves. They were both bigger and more treacherous than the Spaniards had described. The water was cool and rough and tasted slightly sweet. He wondered if the sea captain knew the taste of each ocean. He liked the idea that a conversation that had occurred over two decades ago could still be alive, even if there were only one person left to hear it.

The currents were strong, and he had to use all his skill and energy to duck-dive through the muscular cresting waves. Once he had paddled beyond where they were breaking, he sat on his board for a while to study the patterns of the sets and marvel at the sheer beauty and grace of the lines rolling in—the embodiment of an inevitable perfection. But he couldn't resist for long. The steady rhythm of the waves stilled his mind—he felt the joy that comes from the synchrony of one's body with the rhythm of something more powerful. And for three hours he felt the moods of the ocean.

As the waves twisted over him, he folded down and held his hand out, tracing their inside curves, using touch first to place and then to slow himself down.

When his arms became so heavy from paddling that he lost his lightness, he rode his last wave to shore. Drenched by the beauty and heat of the day, he stretched out on the beach and fell asleep. Some time later he awakened. Based on the position of the sun, he guessed it to be around four o'clock. He went for a swim to wash off the sand before he headed home. He would have missed her for sure, and he wondered why he kept thinking about her. He had learned, long ago, to be indifferent to things that mattered. He had learned to keep hope separated from any sense of happiness.

Alfonso had been worried when Christopher failed to return for lunch. So when he appeared at Casa Tortuga late in the afternoon, he stopped the unnecessary cleaning and nervous readjusting of the pillows. His humming returned, and he offered Señor Christopher a choice for dinner—grilled fish or lobster. He disappeared to start the preparations for the evening meal. Christopher took a long hot shower. Helen would be at LAX heading back to London. He wondered if she were always so buttoned-up—maybe it was a defense, some strong form of resistance against people like Paolo Pavesi. He understood that, too.

He dressed and picked up his book and walked to the *palapa*, where some cold beers and a plate of lime wedges had been left for him. He thought about her again, how he would liked to have had an evening alone with her. But if she had felt what he had felt, she would have found a reason to stay an extra day. He took a long drink of beer and closed his eyes. Feeling so worn out had never felt so good. As he sat there, with the peace that comes from feeling an entire day on his skin and through his muscles and in his bones, he decided he had thought enough about her. As he opened his book, her card dropped out.

CHAPTER FOUR

LONDON

For the three weeks she had been back in London, Helen, like a pilot doing a safety check before takeoff, had gone through all the reasons Christopher should have called her. She hadn't expected to hear anything from him for the first week and a half, because he had said he was staying in Bermeja until the end of January. Had she gone to the correct house? She was certain the jeans she had seen were his. And who else would have been reading about European economics in English? None of the people she had met at Paolo Pavesi's dinner party seemed likely candidates. But Christopher had been content to bring her back to the hotel—he hadn't pushed for anything more, so perhaps that was all there was to it—a casual flirtation that had lost its signal as time elapsed.

She had been thinking all week about lost signals. Her editor had given her the choice between writing a profile of a young art collector who had placed a twenty-foot Jeff Koons sculpture of his iconic balloon dog on his coastline property in Devon or an article on the discovery of a collection of eighteenth-century binders at the Foundling Hospital museum. The binders were filled with records of abandoned babies along with trinkets or pieces of fabric. She had been moved by the trinkets and the small pieces of silks and chintzes and brocades that mothers had attached to their babies' clothing as a means of identifying them in case they returned. She chose to write an article on the discovery of the binders, but it had been more difficult to write than she had anticipated—everything she wrote multiplied the questions to be asked.

When a baby was brought to the Foundling Hospital, a registration billet was created, and mothers were not asked their names but were asked to leave a token of remembrance. The babies were given new names, so the tokens were the only connection to their mothers. Some mothers left trinkets, such as a thimble, a key, a few beads on a fragile cord, a heart-shaped locket, a coin cut in half. Others left strips of material or ribbons, presumably cut from their own clothes. Many of the fragments of fabric had images of hope—birds and butterflies, sprigs with blossoms. One woman left a heart cut out of red fabric pinned to her baby's cap, another the full sleeve of her dress. The ragged pieces of fabric were all that remained of a connection between a mother and a child. One mother left a handwritten poem that ended, "I'd try to have my boy again / And train him up the best of men." The weakness of her hope turned back on itself. She knew she would never see her son again. The ledgers, bloated with filed billets, were shut and rarely opened. The buried connections had no hope of being anything more than lost signals. In many cases Helen was one of the few, if not the first, to examine the billets since their original creation.

She looked back at the letter from the director of the Foundling Hospital museum. The statistics were grim. Two thirds of all the foundlings had died, and many of them had died within days or weeks of being dropped off. She had read that the mortality rate for infants in eighteenth-century London was 50 percent. She wanted to know why the mortality rate was significantly higher at the Foundling Hospital. She wondered if the mothers ever discovered what had happened to their children. The archivist at the museum had very little information. If the children survived, they were apprenticed starting at age eight—the girls for household work, the boys to tradesmen. Of the 16,282 children who had been admitted between 1741 and 1760, only 152 had been reunited with their mothers.

Helen knew she should pull back. Her editor would want the story to be not about the children but about the fragments—what sort of fabric was available in the eighteenth century. These billets provided new information on the type of cloth produced and also gave some indication that it wasn't only working-class mothers who had abandoned their babies. She would have to find a way to combine the two, but it was the fate of the children that obsessed her—as if somehow knowing more could change anything.

Given her word limit, Helen was trying to figure out how to include an image of one of the tokens that did end up being used to unite child and mother. One mother had left a small ditty bag made up of six different postage stamp–size pieces of fabric sewn together. Nine years later, she reclaimed her son with a scrap of matching fabric. Helen stopped and emailed her editor to ask if there were any way she could have more space. He emailed her back and said he would call in five. When the phone rang, she answered, "David, I'm sorry to bring this up at the last minute, but if you could give me room for five hundred or even a thousand more words—I know it's a lot to ask, but I'd like to include—"

"Helen, it's Christopher."

He took her to dinner at her favorite restaurant at the end of the Kings Road and they both ordered *pollo al mattone* and shared a bottle of Gattinara he was pleased to find on the wine list. Instead of catching a taxi home, they walked the three miles back to her flat in Chelsea. It was a typical cold, wet, end-of-January night, with shop windows still advertising sales from the season past. He was surprised when she said she preferred to walk, she wasn't cold or tired. She was—but she wanted to prolong her time with him.

"I'll call you tomorrow about dinner," he said as he kissed her good night. He knew she knew he was teasing her.

"How do you know I'm free?"

"I don't."

He waited for her to open the door before he turned to leave. She was slightly concerned that she liked what he had said as much as she did.

The following evening as they returned from a late dinner at Harry's Bar, he held his hand out for her key, opened the door, took a step back, and then followed her in. There was no question between them about whether he would spend the night. The slow and deliberate way he moved his hands over her body made her feel as if he had been waiting a long time for her. "Are you okay with this?" She nodded and he unbuttoned his shirt. She liked his sense of calm. She would remember thinking that he could do whatever he wanted with her. He kissed her slowly—underneath her neck, across her face, making her wait. She kissed him back. They were on her bed now and he could feel how nervous she was. He outlined her lips with his fingers and traced a line from her mouth down to the dip of her waist to the rise of her hip, his hand moving as if asking questions only her body could answer. He shifted her underneath him and he remembered thinking how light she was—as if all her bones were hollow. She pushed closer into him, he moved through and across her, and she held on and stayed with him. Everything inside her pulled toward the middle, she felt as if she would dissolve completely—but he was holding her together.

CHAPTER FIVE

LONDON

In the morning, she wanted to stay asleep or at least pretend to be asleep until he left, but he woke her up to say good-bye.

"Oh, God," she said, covering her eyes. "I've never done that before."

He looked at her with doubt and amusement.

"No, not that. I mean on the second date."

"Well, I'm glad you did, and for what it's worth, it was our third. Besides, I feel as if I've known you for a long time." He leaned down and kissed her.

He collected his watch from the bedside table. "I have an appointment with an estate agent in an hour to look at flats. Want to come?"

She said she had to finish her article on the Foundling Hospital. Her editor was expecting it by three P.M.

"I'm flying to Paris tonight for a meeting tomorrow, back Wednesday, Thursday at the—Helen, look at me." He held her face in his hands. "I'm not going away." He seemed to know what she was thinking before she did.

He took her phone off the bedside table and added his number to her contacts. "Call me if you finish early. My flight's not until seven."

She already had his number, he had called her. After he left, she looked at her phone. He had replaced Christopher with "Boyfriend" in the contact list and moved it to Favorites.

As Christopher walked down Sloane Avenue, he remembered, in his last year of boarding school, a Russian violin teacher telling him to play a phrase of music as if asking a question and then answering it. In an oblique way, Helen seemed to answer his questions. He had not known what the questions were or even if there were any. Maybe she made the questions unnecessary, like an echo that changed form on its return.

Helen spent the early afternoon fiddling with her article. David had liked what she had written and had agreed to give her the extra space. She sent it off to him and waited for him to give comments. When he emailed back "All set," she was free.

She dressed to go running to prevent herself from calling Christopher. She ran down to Cheyne Walk, across Chelsea Bridge, and around Battersea Park until she could coax herself to run no farther. Exhausted, she turned to walk back to her flat. Thoughts of Christopher seeped back like a slow-moving tide. He was comfortable with himself—maybe because he was older or maybe because he knew where he was going, unlike most of her past boyfriends. Boyfriend? Still, it was more than early days. As she recrossed Chelsea Bridge, she watched the low winter sun glisten the tops of houses before fading down into a dark evening mist. It would be dark by four thirty. He would be on his way to Heathrow.

In Paris, Christopher met with Édouard Beaumont to discuss the textile company that had been owned and run by his family for six generations. Édouard had no heirs, and he was worried that the company was losing market share to Asian imports. He felt it was just a matter of time before the Indians and Chinese would make lace and embroidery almost as well, if not as well, as his company at a quarter of the price. For two days, he had met with bankers and investors from different firms. No one was willing to tell him what Christopher had advised—that he should sell his business, preferably to a high-end French company with a stable of luxury consumer brands.

Christopher understood that most owners knew where they were, they just didn't always know how to make a change or what that change should be. Rarely did anyone understand a business better than the owner, especially those who had grown up in the company. Christopher ran through the scenarios with Édouard. The benefits to being held by a larger French company were many, including a broader marketing platform and financial support in case of a downturn. Not only was Édouard impressed with the cool rationality Christopher offered, but he also liked the expansive way he thought about the business. Most of the other bankers and advisors had recommended bringing in a strategic financial partner, but Édouard knew that a one-time infusion of capital might only delay a decline, not prevent it. Édouard felt that some of the bankers he had interviewed were telling him what they thought he wanted to hear in order to get his business. In the end, he decided to hire the investment professional no one had ever heard of. Christopher stayed an extra day to introduce himself to Édouard's lawyers and accountants.

All the reasons Helen had assembled about her relationship (could she even call it that?) with Christopher not working out—he was nine years older, she had never gone out with anyone remotely connected to business, she didn't fit into his world of high finance, she wasn't fashionable enough—evaporated when she heard his voice. She reversed her position entirely. Mirages of doubt and disbelief that appeared in his absence were dispelled by the sound of his voice saying her name. Why did she feel so safe? He took her on her own terms. He didn't take anything away from her. Didn't look for her to be someone she wasn't. But she didn't even know where he lived. And while it was her nature not to second-guess herself, she understood she had fallen so completely for him that she had no control over what would happen anyway. Besides, when they slept together, they seemed to know each other's bodies before they knew each other. That had to count for something.

Over the weekend, Christopher showed her the townhouse on Birdcage Walk with views of St. James's Park that he and his partner had leased for their office. He was living in the small flat at the top of the building, but he would have to move out soon. The space was needed for the firm's back office and computer equipment. He took her with him the following Sunday to look at more flats. When the real estate agent, to whom he had introduced Helen as his girlfriend, turned her back to silence an alarm, Helen had mouthed, "I'm not your girlfriend," and he had whispered back, "Yes you are," and then had added in a normal voice, "You'll realize this sooner or later."

The flats were either too big or too formal or downright dreary, and Helen suggested that he might want to look at a mews house. The agent knew of one that had just come on the market. It had formerly been part of a stable and was around the corner from Hyde Park. It was small but charming, with an open plan, a bed and bath in what had been the hayloft, and a small garden. Underneath the loft was a small kitchen with stall partitions restored from the original that separated the kitchen from the rest of the ground floor. A second bedroom or study was at the opposite end.

It was furnished with pieces that could have been designed by Andrée Putman. Christopher could go for a run in the park every morning and walk to work in less than twenty minutes. He made an offer that included the furniture, with the condition that he be given an answer by the end of the day.

CHAPTER SIX

LONDON

After a few weeks of seeing each other, Christopher introduced Helen to his business partner. She discovered she had met Marc six months earlier at a drinks party given by her managing editor, David, and his wife, Fernanda. Just as Helen had arrived at 7 Onslow Gardens, a taxi had pulled up and Marc jumped out with a young woman who was thin and petite with long sun-streaked hair. Helen would learn later that her name was Celine and that she and Fernanda had attended art school together. Marc was wearing a European suit without a tie, a starched blue-and-white-striped shirt unbuttoned one more button than any Ivy Leaguer would allow, dark suede driving shoes without socks. Celine was holding a flower in her hand and looked bored.

The party was being held on the second floor and a number of guests had spilled through French doors onto the balcony facing the street. As they waited underneath the portico, Marc got impatient that no one was answering the door. Either someone had mistakenly locked the ground-floor door or the noise of the party was so loud that the buzzer could not be heard. He hurried to the sidewalk and yelled up to the guests on the balcony. His brash and arrogant behavior, behavior that Helen had come across and disliked in most of the American investment bankers she had met in London, had more to do with theatrics than self-absorption. When someone finally did appear, Helen was unable to hold her prejudice for long because, as Marc held the door open for her, he swept his arm sideways and bowed to "m'lady." And she would remember the way he reached for his girlfriend's hand—as if he always knew where it would be. Helen never got a chance to see her again. Marc told her that a month after the drinks party, Celine had returned from Brussels wearing a man's watch that wasn't his.

In the first six months, Christopher and Marc's business was harder to get started than they had imagined. They had met in New York, first on opposite sides of a deal and then on the same side. Christopher was a junior partner at one of the top law firms specializing in corporate finance, and Marc was a vice president at one of the major investment banks. When Marc had decided to set up his own firm, Christopher was the first person he had approached about joining him. He was impressed with Christopher and thought they would complement each other. And they did. Marc hustled for new business and brought Christopher in when the client wanted to be convinced further. They began with advisory work, and once they were established, planned to expand into principal investing and fund management.

But in the early days they fought hard for each piece of new business, and they lost more than they won. Corporations were risk averse and hiring their firm was judged riskier than working with Morgan Stanley or Goldman Sachs or JPMorgan. Entrepreneurs who were comfortable with risk hired them first. They understood that Christopher and Marc went to sleep worrying about their deal—a disposition rare among bankers at the established firms, where lists of transactions were always waiting to be done.

Unlike their competitors, Christopher and Marc did not have the luxury of losing.

With a few deals behind them, they had started building the track record they needed. For Christopher, work was the thing he could lose himself in but never lose any part of himself. If a deal or negotiation got off track, it could never cripple him, never pull him under. He had an ability to see how a negotiation would play out with a skill that was rare. Marc had his own talent for getting business. Entrepreneurs, especially the ones who had learned to create their own opportunities, liked him. They saw something of themselves in him, and they had a softness for the young man who was a little too brash and a little too unpolished, but whose energy for what he was doing was irresistible. He literally hurled himself against any opportunity, as if he were trying to break down a door.

In the beginning, it was just the two of them, a shared secretary, and a young Brit with a doctorate in computer sciences, too brilliant and too rough for an established firm, who doubled as researcher and IT architect. Christopher and Marc went after business, chased down leads, asked for introductions, made cold calls. The energy spent during the day was sustained through the evening. It was as if those laid-back days in Bermeja had never existed. Helen often met Christopher at his office on Birdcage Walk for a late dinner after work. On the evenings she waited for him, she could not tell the hour by the level of activity. The buzz of the office was nonstop. After less than a year, the firm had grown to fifteen professionals plus support staff. Somewhere a phone was always ringing. The associates ran, never walked, down corridors. Helen watched what the *Financial Times* had called the hottest financial advisory boutique in Europe grow as if a slow-speed camera had been put on fast-forward.

On Saturdays, Christopher and Helen spent the day together, going to exhibits, running errands, occasionally meeting one of his colleagues or clients for dinner. If she had to finish an article, he would make her coffee and wait for her. Only once or twice did they have dinner with one of his friends from boarding school or university. He brought little forward from the past. Sometimes he stayed with her, but mostly she stayed with him. When she heard from an old school friend that her sister's young daughter needed open-heart surgery in London, Christopher suggested that Helen give the sister her flat.

"You said she needed a place to stay in London and money is an issue, so why don't you move in with me? If you want to move back in a month, I promise I will release you," he said. "But as you and I both know, unlike in Cinderella, around here, all the great things take place after midnight." She threw a pillow at him but followed his plan.

CHAPTER SEVEN

SUSSEX

With three older brothers who rarely thought much about their younger sister until she had a boyfriend, bringing a date to one of her mother's Sunday lunches was something Helen rarely looked forward to—the subtle and not-so-subtle questions and then the aftermath of inquiry when her relationship faltered or hit a bad patch or just simply crashed. But most of all, she dreaded her three sisters-in-law, who always felt it was their duty to assist in the recovery efforts, which they interpreted as setting her up with a friend's brother or cousin. This time, however, would be different. It would be the first time she had brought a boyfriend who was neither a journalist nor a "between assignments" photographer and who was more accomplished than her brothers. There would not be the awkward spaces as there were last time when her mother and Celia, her middle brother's wife, tried to understand what interest her last boyfriend had in photographs of crime scenes overlaid with Gerhard Richter–like wavy lines of paint. She knew the minute she and this photographer left, the question for anyone who remained was "Where does Helen find them?" And when these short-lived romantic attachments were over, even Helen found herself wondering about her propensity for miscalculation.

"So you grew up in Sussex?" Christopher asked as he unlocked her car and opened the door for her.

"Are you sure you want to drive? We're going on the M3. Right-hand drive is not as easy as it looks."

"Remember, I went to school here."

"I know, but presumably—"

"You'll be okay. Promise. So always West Sussex?"

"Yes, I was born there. Both Theo and I were. Louis and Max were born in London at Guy's and St. Thomas', where—little-known fact—Keats trained as a surgeon. When my mother was expecting Theo, my parents moved to the country."

Willow Brook was a lovely eighteenth-century manor house set in the South Downs several miles west of the village of Petworth. When Christopher and Helen arrived, her parents, brothers, sisters-in-law, nieces, and nephews were sitting in the garden. It was one of those rare and glorious sunny days in early June. As they approached, Helen's concerns reversed themselves. She became anxious about what Christopher would think of her family. Would he find her brothers, two of whom worked in the country, too English and provincial?

Christopher had no such worries, nor did he feel he needed to know anything more about Helen. Rather, it was the abnormally normal setting that absorbed his attention. No matter how many times he encountered family gatherings, the thought *So this is how families unbroken by deaths and divorces behave* recurred like an unwelcome refrain.

Helen introduced Christopher to her mother and father and then to her three brothers and their wives—Henrietta, Celia, and Emma. The children who were playing on the lawn by the pool were called over to give Aunt Helen a kiss and to shake hands with Christopher. Louis offered them a Pimm's Cup. Helen's mother was keen to know about Christopher's family, and he explained that his mother had grown up in the States but had lived in Europe most of her life. His father was French and had died in a skiing accident when he was young. His mother had moved to London for the years he and his sister attended English boarding schools but then moved back to France once they were at university. When the conversation shifted to questions about his work, Helen's mother left with Celia, who went to check on her sleeping baby. Mrs. Gibbs promised to return after she checked on the roast chickens.

At lunch, Christopher was seated between Helen's mother and her middle brother, Max. Helen was seated at the other end of the table with two of her sisters-in-law, who were commiserating over nursery schools. Her father sat quietly and spoke to his eldest son about his recent trip to Beijing, where his firm was setting up an office. Helen glanced at Christopher, who was listening to her mother describe how Petworth House, along with a few other grand Grade I properties in the surrounding area, had been turned into a school during World War II. He caught her eye and smiled in a way that told her all was calm. When lunch was over, everyone moved to the library for coffee. Louis and her father approached Christopher and asked if he'd had any dealings with the Chinese. She overheard him saying something about having worked on the sale of a minority interest to a Chinese conglomerate when he was practicing law in New York.

From across the room, Christopher could feel Helen's edginess. Her family had never lived past the borders of England. Her father was a partner in a small law firm specializing in trusts and estates, her mother occupied herself with her garden and her grandchildren. Christopher knew they would have concerns about their daughter bringing home a boyfriend who was half American, half French, almost ten years older, and whom they would be unable to place in any category. He knew that her brothers—a lawyer, a chartered accountant, and an estate manager—were expecting the stereotypical investment banker—arrogant, smug, taken with himself. He was safe from these charges. Maybe because he had moved around so much, he had learned to listen—to understand where he was before he offered much.

Theo invited Christopher to join him on one of the shoots his firm managed, but Christopher politely demurred, saying such an invitation would be wasted on him, he wasn't a particularly good shot and didn't own a gun. He added that starting a firm had been harder than he had expected, and he was having to spend all his time getting it off the ground. Emma, on learning that he had recently bought a small mews house, and not knowing that Helen was living with him, was offering the design services of one of her dearest friends, when Louis and Henrietta's daughter, Leonora, flew into the library, partly crying, partly shrieking two words—*helicopter* and *Caspar*. In the way that only children can, she had the entire room of adults standing at attention. Louis and Henrietta calmed their eight-year-old daughter enough to learn that five-year-old Henry had been flying his toy helicopter, and when Leonora had gone into the paddock to see Helen's ancient pony, Caspar, the crafty pony had taken off across the south field. Louis and Helen followed Leonora to Caspar's paddock to confirm his escape. Leonora held on to a vague belief that Henry's helicopter had caused the pony to bolt and that he had done it on purpose.

They weren't sure where Caspar had gone, but they were fearful he could be heading over to the neighboring property, where he was kept and fed during the winter months. He would have to cross a stretch of road that could be busy at this time in June.

"I know the way he'll go. Christopher and I can drive down to the crossroads." Helen started to run toward the barn.

"Helen, where are you going?" Louis called out.

"To get some grain and a halter," she called back.

Helen showed Christopher which way to go, but before they got to the crossroads, she spotted Caspar in a field full of grass and cows.

"There he is. That little devil. You can pull over there." She pointed to a grassy area by the road.

"Here, give me the halter," he said. She ran across the road and slipped between the rails of the fencing. Christopher followed at a slower pace with the rope and halter hidden behind his back. Caspar saw Helen coming, jerked his head up, snorted, gave a little buck, and trotted sixty feet away. She stayed where she was and shook the bucket of grain. Caspar edged closer. Soon the shaggy, once-white pony was pushing his mouth into the bucket of food. Christopher slowly approached and wrapped the rope around the pony's neck. When Caspar realized what had happened, he attempted to back up, rear, and twist away, but Christopher held him tight. "He's a tough little devil," he said as he slipped the halter over the pony's head.

"You've been around horses before," she said, somewhat surprised. He shrugged. "A bit." She was so preoccupied with the unruly pony that she didn't have time to ask another question.

"I'll walk him home. You know the way back?" Caspar pushed her hard to try to get to the feed bucket.

"Here, give me that." Christopher reached for the bucket of grain. "Straight ahead for a bit and then right at first turning."

Caspar tried to charge toward the transferred bucket of grain. "You sure you don't want me to come—he's really full of himself."

"If I could handle him when I was twelve, I should be able to handle him now."

Helen returned to Willow Brook with Caspar, and Leonora, who had been worried she would never see Caspar again, was offered a pony ride to cheer her up. Henry was banished with his helicopter to the front lawn on the other side of the house.

CHAPTER EIGHT

SAINT-TROPEZ

Helen never moved back into her flat. She had a small mortgage left, so she let it out short term to friends or friends of friends. As Christopher's mews house began to feel more like theirs and less like his, she became less and less concerned about the duration of the lease. Her work was going well, and David was giving her more scope to choose her topics—one even came from Christopher's world—the profile of a successful music company entrepreneur who was dedicating his time and considerable fortune to his NGO fostering entrepreneurs in sub-Saharan Africa.

At first she found the world in which Christopher worked intriguing. The parameters were always changing. A quiet weekend in London could be redirected to Berlin to see a client, or, as was the case on Friday, a weekend in the country was overwritten with an invitation to Saint-Tropez. She could tell how fast Christopher's star was rising by how many invitations he received from people he did not know. She found it odd that people they had never met invited them to dinners and parties and sporting events. In her world, friendships were slow to form, but in Christopher and Marc's world, access was instant. Friends of friends were assumed to be friends, and invitations were extended. Their world was small and select, but once access was granted, barriers evaporated. It was as if a certain category of person did away with the need for introductions and periods of engagement necessary to make acquaintances. She could only assume there was a layer of society that was unapologetic in its admiration of money and influence. Marc, much more than Christopher, worked this aspect to his advantage. Christopher was disciplined enough never to turn down an invitation that could lead to more business for his firm. At first she enjoyed the invitations, but often she found herself watching events alone while Christopher had a private conversation with a chief executive who pulled him away to run an idea by him or get his reaction to a recent business story. She knew she would never run into any of her friends.

At first the choice between spending the weekend at the country house of one of her friends or attending a dinner with a new client was easy. Christopher always assumed priority, and if she questioned him, he would say he didn't have a choice. But over time, she began missing her old life. Not that any weekend was going to be anything special, but she missed the menagerie of former classmates from boarding school and university—most of whom had pursued careers without regard for how little money they would be making a decade out. Money and possessions were never discussed, because no one had much. Often she came across ideas for articles to run by David. Her article about the Chevalier d'Éon, the French diplomat and spy who infiltrated the court of Empress Elizabeth of Russia by presenting himself as a woman, had come from a classmate who now taught history at Stowe. Another friend, who worked for the London Arts Council, had told Helen about a prima ballerina who wanted to meet the maker of her pointe shoes.

As was the custom of all the makers, he identified himself only by an initial stamped on the sole of each shoe. Despite David's misgivings, Helen had accompanied the dancer to the north of England to track down "J." Instead of finding an elflike man in a charming cottage, they met a young, hip black man who lived on a council estate and who had never been to the ballet. He followed football. For him, it was just a job, one he had fallen into by chance when he had dropped out of school at age fourteen.

Had there not been these undercurrents, Helen would have been thrilled when Christopher returned from work Friday evening and said they were going to Saint-Tropez the following day so that he could meet with his client, Édouard Beaumont. They flew to Nice and took a helicopter to Saint-Tropez, where Édouard met them at the heliport and drove them in his Mini Moke to La Mandala, the villa built by his grandfather at the turn of the century. La Mandala sat on the flat top of a hill that sloped sharply down to the Mediterranean Sea. A pool and a terraced garden sprawled behind the one-story villa, which had been built around an open courtyard. From La Mandala, one could walk along the shoreline into town and be seated at an outdoor café in fifteen minutes.

Édouard showed Helen the pool and library. He and Christopher retreated to his study to discuss the details of the sale of his company. She went for a swim but soon became bored and changed back into her clothes and wandered into the library. Rows and rows of uniform leather-bound volumes in French and German—histories and biographies, mainly—all in perfect formation as if they had marched into place. She skimmed along the rows looking for any books in English. She found a small collection in one of the darkest corners of the room. A four-volume edition of Churchill's *A History of the English-Speaking Peoples*, *Moby-Dick*, and a slim volume, *Ins and Outs of Circus Life*. She edged the slight volume from the shelf, careful not to pull the cloth at the top of the spine. She was about to open it when Édouard and Christopher appeared.

"Ah, I see you've found my orphaned book," Édouard said, taking the book from her. "It's the only book in this library not catalogued by my father. I can only assume a guest from a long time ago left it behind. But how it got here, no one will ever know. It's quite rare, that one, one of only twelve known. I keep meaning to donate it to a museum of circus life, if such a thing exists. But come, I have kept Christopher away from you for too long. I will drive you to your hotel."

Hotel Byblos was just down the hill from La Mandala. On the drive down, Édouard told Helen that Christopher had mentioned her article on the binders discovered at the Foundling Hospital museum. His family had been in the textile industry before the French Revolution. He would be interested to see the documentation of the fabrics from the 1700s. She must send him a copy of her article, and he would let her know if any of the fabrics were French.

Édouard met them in town later that evening to take them to a chic Moroccan restaurant decorated with cushions of brightly colored, beaded ethnic textiles and handsome waiters, all of whom looked as if they had just walked off a fashion runway. Over dinner, Helen asked Édouard about the history of La Mandala. He explained that his grandfather had bought the land when it was nothing but the foundation of a former fortress.

"My grandmother would have liked a bigger house, but my grandfather refused to build beyond the footprint of the fortress. He felt the spirits of the place would only approve a design that reflected the past. My grandfather was a very superstitious man. I have been coming here every summer since I was born, as had my father before me. But after Christopher sells my company, I am going to sail around the world. It has always been a boyhood dream of mine."

"How long will that take?" Helen asked.

"Depends."

"Approximately." Christopher stepped in to cut off Édouard's attempt to flirt with her.

"Four to six months with a very good boat and a very good team, but I plan to take my time. I like the idea of stretching it over one year. I would like to end on the same day that I began."

"But you'll miss your summer at La Mandala," she said.

"Yes, but perhaps the break will be good. I have spent every summer of my sixty-one years here. It is time I take a mistress for one of them. What about you?" he asked Christopher and Helen. "Did your family take you to the same place every year? It's a very English thing to do, no?"

Christopher turned to Helen for her to speak first.

"No, not really. We pretty much stayed in England—in the country. A few summers we visited one of my mother's cousins in Scotland or a friend on the Isle of Wight."

"And you, Christopher? Have you noticed, Helen, how well Christopher listens and how he never answers first. It is a sign of a good negotiator."

Christopher laughed.

"You see, he is not going to answer the question."

They said good night to Édouard. It was past one A.M., and Byblos was in full swing. Outside, Ferraris and Maseratis and other fancy cars were prominently displayed; inside, young women in expensive dresses drank and danced with men who were almost as attractive as they were. Helen marveled at the sense of glamour that surrounded them. *What do these people do during the day?* she wondered. Christopher stopped by reception to get their room key, and the manager offered them a complimentary glass of champagne at the bar, but Christopher declined. He and Helen only wanted to be with each other.

CHAPTER NINE

FONTAINEBLEAU

Early Sunday afternoon they flew from Nice to Paris, rented a car, and drove south to Fontainebleau, where Christopher's mother lived at the edge of the forest. Soon they were on a road that paralleled the Seine. "You can take a boat from Paris all the way," he said.

"Have you ever done it?"

"No, but I remember my father talking about it."

Christopher circled back to the edge of the forest and turned down an unpaved road. He slowed to pass two riders who trotted in single file. A few miles later he turned down a road that distinguished itself by a formal avenue of plane trees. They passed a small gatehouse. "Just there"—he pointed to a rise in the land several hundred feet ahead—"was the main house, but it burned down and was never rebuilt." He turned down a secondary road and followed its slow curve through the woods.

"Here we are." He parked in front of a one-story building with a flat roof.

A tall thin woman opened the door. Christopher's mother. Two large tan-and-black dogs that vaguely resembled lions stood beside her. Mrs. Delavaux's face was softer than Helen had imagined. The lack of a strong correspondence between mother and son made Helen wonder about Christopher's father.

They entered a small vestibule and then a large rectangular room with high ceilings. "This was my mother's studio. I don't know if Christopher showed you, but there was a massive house at the end of the main avenue." Mrs. Delavaux's voice was soft, and Helen had to lean forward to hear her.

"It had been built by my mother's older sister. She and her husband never had children, and in the twenties they decided to leave Tuxedo Park and build a house here. She dabbled a bit in art, but I think she built the studio for my mother after her divorce. I remember coming here when I was little."

Helen looked around. Paintings—mainly of landscapes, a few portraits—were hung in organized randomness around the room.

"All the pictures are hers—I think she was a wonderful painter—amateur only, of course. She kept most of what she did, but she did give a few away to friends. I'm glad she kept most of them. They comfort me. To be around her work. When my aunt died, she left this property to me. We moved here when Christopher was just learning to walk. The year Christopher went off to boarding school, the main house burned down. We never learned how the fire started, but the police think some people who were living rough in the forest left their campfire unattended.

"We always talked about building the main house back, didn't we, Christopher?" Mrs. Delavaux glanced at her son, who was gazing out into the garden. "But I think it was more out of a sense of the past than anything else. And of course we never did—what use would I have of a massive fourteen-bedroom house? After Christopher and Laure went off to school, they only came back for parts of the summer. I never thought I would live here as long as I have, but here I am. And of course I have all my animals." She rubbed the ears of the two large dogs sitting next to her. "Oh, dear, I'm prattling on. Now, Helen, Christopher tells me you're a writer."

"A journalist. I write features for the *Sunday Times* in London."

A housekeeper brought in a tray of tea and biscuits.

"Let's have tea in the garden and then we'll go for a walk. I'll show you the stables and the two foals born at the beginning of May."

Christopher had learned how to navigate these encounters with his mother by steering away from anything that could conjure the past. He had his reasons for staying away from certain topics. Maybe it helped his mother to fall backward, but it didn't help him, and he knew, too, that if his response wasn't as she desired, there would be sound waves of small antagonisms and minor hurts.

Helen watched as Mrs. Delavaux poured tea from a silver teapot that had a top inlaid with a cabochon emerald.

"It's beautiful, isn't it? It was made by Puiforcat as a wedding gift for my parents. Now, Helen, what do you take in your tea?"

"Milk and sugar, please."

She handed Helen a cup and then offered a small silver tray of biscuits.

As they stood up to walk to the stable, Christopher excused himself to make some phone calls. Mrs. Delavaux and Helen walked down to the small stone stable built in the same style as the studio. Mrs. Delavaux spoke about how busy the stable had been when they all rode. "When we had twelve horses, the barn was always so wonderfully warm, even when it was snowing outside." She pointed to the two foals who shadowed their mothers in the pasture.

"I have a girl who comes and will start working with them next year. Just to get them used to being handled."

"What are their names?"

"Dea is the small bay filly and the large chestnut colt is Serengeti. Do you ride?"

"Oh, I did, just around the countryside on a renegade pony. Nothing serious."

"When they turn three, I send them on to a wonderful man who breaks and trains them, and then, if they have promise, I let one of the young professional riders take them on."

"Where do they show?"

"Mainly in France. Occasionally in Belgium or Holland. I've only had a few with the ability to compete on the international level. But it's great fun to go and watch them. Christopher's father was a wonderful rider. As a young man he rode on the French national team. He always said Christopher had three times his talent. As I imagine you know, when he was fourteen he won a grand prix at Val-de-Reuil, the youngest rider ever to do so. He had huge promise, but one day at age fifteen he just stopped."

"We should go." Christopher stood up when his mother and Helen walked into the house. He tilted his watch toward him. "Our flight leaves in three hours."

"Oh, Christopher, I do wish you would stay."

"We can't. I have to fly to Edinburgh first thing in the morning."

"Why didn't you tell me you were such a good rider?" Helen asked as they drove back to Orly.

"I wasn't that good. My mother only remembers the highlights. Laure was the real talent, but she doesn't ride anymore. I had a sort of go-for-broke style. When you're fourteen, with nothing to lose, you can get away with that."

"But she said you won an international—"

"I had a really good horse." He cut her off and checked his rear-view mirror. He switched lanes to pass a lorry.

"Why did you stop?"

"Oh, I don't know, other things I wanted to do, I guess."

"Your mother is sweet."

"She is, but she's complicated."

"She seems lonely."

"Maybe, but everything has to be on her terms. Her friends are always people she collects or feels sorry for. She finds talented working students and gives them good horses to ride, and that works for a while until she feels they have been disloyal or unappreciative, and then that relationship falters. I've learned over the years to stay out of it."

As they were boarding their flight, Édouard called Christopher to discuss a few more points about the sale of his company. He also made it clear he only wanted to deal with Christopher and not the junior vice president assigned to his company. It was just as well. Trying to get Édouard to understand that his high-end textile company was not worth as much as he thought would take time. Christopher knew that no matter how talented his junior associate was, his opinion would never be accepted by Édouard. Christopher mulled over in his mind the best way to structure the sale. He had a small list of high-quality buyers. An auction with buyers bidding against each other would be ideal. He would have to give more thought to whether such a process was realistic.

Helen looked out the window and thought about what they did and didn't know about each other. Why was Christopher holding things back? Was he holding things back? She couldn't answer either question. When they reached home, he asked her what was bothering her. He had learned to read her moods.

"Nothing. Nothing's bothering me."

"Come on, you're going to be like this until you tell me, so let's get it over with."

"You're being so patronizing."

"Practical. Come on, tell me."

"It's just that you make me feel unsettled."

"I make you feel unsettled? How?" He laughed.

"Christopher, don't laugh at me."

"I'm not laughing at you. It's just that I find your comment silly. Okay"—he softened his voice and looked directly at her—"how do I make you feel unsettled?"

"I feel we're speaking on this level." She moved her hands across an imaginary horizontal line. "But there's this whole other world going on below that's unreachable, inaccessible."

"You know you're suggesting an alternative universe."

"Christopher, stop, please. We've known each other for just over six months. It's been intense. But as close as you and I have become, there are parts of your life—your family, for example—that I know nothing about. You never told me you were a good rider. Doesn't that strike you as odd?"

"No. It just didn't come up."

"Oh, come on, Christopher. You know what I'm saying."

"I didn't tell you because it's not important to me. That's all. Listen, I have to leave tomorrow at four A.M. I can't get into this conversation now. Let's have it when I get back."

"Is it always going to be like this?"

"Like what?"

"Are you always going to have to work so hard?"

"Helen, I don't know what to say. I committed to starting a firm. I have people working for me who are depending on me. They have mortgages and families. Once you're in the river, you're in the river. You can't get out and take a break. Right now I know it's hard on you. It's not always going to be like this, but it is for a while. When a client asks me to come see him, I don't have the luxury of saying no. We need every piece of business we can get."

"It just feels like you're trying to run a three-ring circus sometimes."

"I understand. It feels like that to me, too, but I have only one option, and that is to keep the rings going and the clients happy. At some point my firm will get to a point where I can turn over more of the business to others. But we're not there yet."

Christopher called the following day. His meeting had gone well, and he had been asked to give his thoughts on the preliminary valuation of a subsidiary that the company was considering selling. He was going to stay in Edinburgh to do the necessary due diligence. He would be home late Friday evening. In his absence, Helen met up with friends for dinner, friends like Peregrine, who had started at the paper the same time she had but who had left his position as a junior member of the obituary department to write a biography of an obscure, but distinguished, ancestor. And Zara, who worked at the Royal Society of Literature and wrote book reviews on the side. Helen and her friends had always noticed when a boyfriend or girlfriend took one of their group away. It happened when Peregrine's twin sister, Flora, began seeing a much older writer or when another friend started seeing a young woman who had never finished university and was, by anyone's description, spoiled and not very bright. These attachments meant they weren't coming back because their partners were incompatible with the group. In the months she had been seeing Christopher, Helen had rarely thought about including him with her friends. If anything, she avoided them until he was away. She told herself it was because he wouldn't understand any of the inside jokes and the gossip. He wouldn't know any of the history knitting them together. But she also knew she behaved a little differently when she was with him. And she knew her friends would notice, too.

CHAPTER TEN

BERMEJA

For Christmas, Christopher gave Helen a necklace—a thin gold strand with a faceted aquamarine in the shape of a teardrop. He told her to pack enough clothes for ten days under a hot sun. He would not tell her where they were going, but the watery light blue color of the stone was a clue. Helen was thrilled with the idea of going away for Christmas week. She had very little pressing work, and the dreary darkness of December days and rain-sogged evenings were just setting in. Her brothers and their families alternated Christmas between the sets of grandparents, and this year Louis and Theo had planned to spend Christmas at Willow Brook. Christopher seemed to operate on an understanding that families required only the minimum of commitments, but Helen did wonder if she would be missed.

The journey to Bermeja was long. They flew from London to Los Angeles and took a connecting flight to Puerto Vallarta. From there Christopher chartered a small prop plane to take them the two hundred miles south to Bermeja. He offered Helen the seat next to the pilot, but when she saw the pedals, she decided to sit in the back. She would have been happier driving. She liked to drive distances, especially if they were long, but he was always impatient to get where he was going as quickly as possible. The pilot explained it was faster to fly straight south across the peninsula of land, but she asked if they could fly along the coast. He shrugged acquiescence but told her there was nothing to see but miles and miles of uninhabited beaches. Christopher wondered if he were the same pilot he had seen the day he first met Helen.

The sun was shining and the wind was strong. The small plane slipped and bounced and slapped across pockets of air, and Helen thought there was no way the wings would not break off. The pilot hunched his shoulders and leaned forward, as if by doing so he would be able to see the rough patches of wind. There was a reason they had not seen any fishing boats that day.

When they stepped off the plane, the unyielding solidness of the ground felt almost foreign. Alfonso was waiting in a jeep in the shade of the coconut grove that separated the landing strip from the polo field. They drove along the coast and up the cliff to Casa Tortuga.

"This place makes you see things differently," Christopher said.

They stood on the terrace and watched the wind chasing archipelagos of clouds across the sky. Shadows of cobalt blue were sliding along the surface of the turquoise sea. It was as if all the bright colors had run away and now were found. She watched a bright green iguana pause on cocked elbows before disappearing under a bush of pink bougainvillea. They could hear the waves breaking on the rocks below.

"I remember the first time I came here. My mother brought us for Christmas the year my father died. She wanted to be as far away from the Alps as possible. The first night I couldn't sleep—probably some combination of missing my father and jet lag. My mother told me to listen for the moment each wave paused before pulling back from the shore."

"Did it work?"

"Eventually."

"I'm not sure I can tell," she said. "It almost sounds like a plane that doesn't get any closer."

"If you listen long enough you'll be able to hear it."

They unpacked and sat outside and watched the day disappear.

"I have a theory," she said, remembering everything about her first encounter with Christopher a year ago. "I think that emotions experienced in a place stay where they are, and when you come back you encounter them, you find them again. It's why coming back here feels so strong. It's not memory, but feeling." She tried hard to persuade him of her theory, but he laughed, and she could tell he would not allow himself to believe such things.

"You are aware that your theories about invisible things are not supported by any laws of physics."

"No, really, Christopher, I'm serious. I think at some point scientists will discover that there are waves of energy between all of us. And that we know more than we allow ourselves to know."

Even though he didn't believe her theories about emotions being left in a place and currents connecting people—no matter where they were—he liked being with someone who did.

The following day, their plans for a long walk dissipated into reading by the pool. Through the parallel wooden slats of a pergola, the sun sliced shadows across Christopher's back.

"You might end up looking like a keyboard or a convict if you stay where you are," she said as she shook his arm to awaken him from an afternoon nap. He picked up his book from where it had fallen.

"That would only be good if the dinner tonight were a costume party," he said as he moved his chaise close to hers.

In the week between Christmas and New Year's Day, Bermeja was in full swing, with most of the owners of the houses in residence. A number of handwritten invitations from people they had vaguely heard of but had never met were dropped off by staff.

"How did anyone know we were coming?" she asked. "Does Philippe spend Christmas here with his father?"

"Marc said he was going skiing with him in Courchevel. I don't think Philippe comes here that often." Helen was not surprised that Marc was going skiing—it was just the type of Christmas holiday she would expect him to take—but she was surprised he was going with Philippe, and she was surprised Christopher had not told her. She was not aware that Marc and Philippe knew each other.

The first dinner party they attended was given by Henri and Penelope Lartigue, a French businessman and his artist wife. Henri was the CEO of his family's chemical company, one of the largest privately held companies in Europe. The Lartigues' saffron-colored house was perched on top of a cliff with an infinity pool wrapped so tightly around it that their house appeared to be floating. A six-foot-wide wooden bridge gave access to the house. Christopher and Helen arrived just as the evening turned indigo. They joined the other guests on the terrace overlooking the pool to the Pacific Ocean. Penelope introduced them to a very tall woman with gray hair pulled back tight in a chignon. Helen recognized the woman's surname as one of the most influential families in Germany.

They were soon called to dinner in the large circular space covered by a soaring *palapa*. They found their names painted on shells around a table that seated sixteen. They were asked to join hands, and the hostess gave a simple blessing. Both Helen and Christopher, independent of one another, tried to remember the last time they had been to church.

Helen sat between an elderly American writer and a titled Austrian whose family owned a sporting gun company. Not being well enough informed about the writer's reputation as a curmudgeon, she asked him how he had learned to write. "By copying other writers," he said. "Flaubert in particular." He told her that when he understood how Flaubert had created the scene in which Emma Bovary is at the dance and decides how unhappy she is with her life, he knew he had become a writer. "If you can figure out how to do that, if you understand that, then you know how to write." She asked him if he wrote every day. "No, of course not," he said, but she wasn't sure she believed him. The Austrian count asked Helen if she had given up skiing. He had—now he sought the sun on holidays. He spoke to her as if he were placing large pieces of luggage on a conveyor belt.

Christopher sat between Penelope and the fourth wife of a Swiss art dealer, a tall young Asian woman. Christopher enjoyed speaking with Penelope. She was a photographer, and while she spent more time on the decoration of her seven houses than on her photography, she had resisted the clichéd hallmarks of the wealthy wife and dressed in a bohemian style. At the end of the evening she balanced a glass of wine on her head and took a picture of everyone. The wife of the art dealer was younger than her husband's youngest daughter. When Christopher turned to speak to her, she introduced herself by saying, "I know how to say, 'Are we having fun or what?' in thirteen different languages." In rough English, she bragged that she made her soon-to-be-octogenarian husband work out every day with her personal trainer. As she spoke, Christopher thought that if she, instead of Eve, had been in the Garden of Eden, she would have eaten the snake.

The hostess stood up and directed the guests to the jeeps that would take them to Paolo Pavesi's end-of-year celebration. Helen waited for Christopher to finish his conversation with Henri. She had been around the office enough to know that being able to pick up the phone and reach the owner of Europe's largest private chemical company was an opportunity he would not let pass. The wind was picking up and the air was cooling. Far away from shore, a small yellow light bobbed frenetically. Fishermen, she thought. She felt safe being where she was. The ocean was rough, with the prophecy of a storm.

They had decided against going to Paolo's end-of-year party, but when they learned that the party was being held at his inverted temple, they could not resist. They followed the caravan of jeeps the four miles to a strip of land that jutted out into the ocean. On the drive, Helen thought about this collection of people gathered on the last days of the year. There was an exclusivity about this world, and she wasn't sure she liked it. Assumptions were made, exceptions were granted, a formal intimacy was expected. Maybe over time it would feel more natural, though she doubted it. She suspected she would never see any of these people again. Christopher might. Knowing some of these families could produce deals and advisory work. But it was a world elevated from transactions. Nothing would be mentioned here. Marc was too rough for this world. It demanded an ease, a comfort with nuance, and it required its own form of patience. *Sprezzatura*? Christopher's ability to navigate so effortlessly confirmed his ease in a three-ring circus world. Maybe he did not wish to belong exclusively to any of them. Maybe it was his way of creating an anonymity he cherished.

The large concrete bowl, ringed with diamond-shaped windows at three-foot intervals, was three stories high and almost a third of a football field in diameter. A wooden staircase steadied by X-shaped supports rose to the top of the rim. A few of the guests chose to climb the stairs to walk around the perimeter of the bowl; others followed Paolo through an opening at the bottom of the structure. Christopher, who had climbed to the top before, had never been inside so he steered Helen toward Paolo. Once inside, Paolo asked everyone to lie down and regard the moon. He had asked a poet from France to give a reading. The young women who perpetually orbited Paolo brought pillows for everyone. The night sky was glorious, and everyone was soothed by the pulse of the waves, as if the heartbeat of the world.

Paolo stood in the middle of the circle and spoke in a combination of Italian, Spanish, and French. He switched languages as if skipping stones across water. He introduced the poet, who said he was going to recite Baudelaire's poem "*Tristesses de la lune*." The poet, whom neither Helen nor Christopher had heard of, spoke slowly and deliberately. When he had finished, Paolo asked him to repeat the last stanza. He obliged.

Dans le creux de sa main prend cette larme pâle,
Aux reflets irisés comme un fragment d'opale,
Et la met dans son coeur loin des yeux du soleil.

In a quiet voice, Christopher translated for Helen.

In the hollow of his hand catches this pale tear,
With the iridescent reflections of a fragment of opal,
And hides it in his heart far from the sun's eyes.

Paolo stood up and spoke. Christopher continued to translate. "He is asking everyone to find any sadness we have buried in our hearts and to offer it to the moon tonight—something about the moon drinking our tears of sadness—and to leave everything behind and to enter the new year with a heart cleansed of unhappiness."

Paolo ended the evening with a version of a benediction. "Let us praise the colors of the land and the sun and the sky. As Kandinsky said, 'Color directly influences the soul.' Without the color-drenched earth, we have only tears that the moon must take away. And let us always return, let our souls always migrate, no matter where we find ourselves, like the sea turtles, to this blessed place."

"That was not at all what I was expecting," Christopher said to

Helen as they walked back to their jeep. He knew she was thinking the same. He thought about her word *neverness*. He wondered how Baudelaire would have used it.

"Do you believe what he said about colors?" she asked.

"You mean about their influence on the soul? I do. I read somewhere that one in two thousand people hears colors. For that person, the sound of a color is as certain and distinct as a musical note. The French composer Messiaen saw colors when he heard or imagined music."

She considered what he had said. "I wonder what this world would have sounded like to him." When he didn't respond, she added, "Paolo really loves this place, doesn't he?"

"He does."

"More than his family?"

"Probably. It's his life's work."

"Do you really believe that?"

"I do. But first you have to ask if he is even capable of loving another person. Some people aren't."

CHAPTER ELEVEN

BERMEJA

The following day, the sun seduced all thoughts away. A polo match had been scheduled for the late afternoon, and Christopher and Helen had been invited. The polo field was within walking distance, just one coconut grove from the grass landing strip, but for Christopher and Helen, the sun had not followed the orders of the day, and they arrived just as the last chukker was being played. When the game was over, they stopped by the hotel bar for a cold drink before climbing the steep road to Casa Tortuga. A beautifully turned-out, mildly overweight woman came rushing up, shrieking Christopher's name with the delight of someone who had just won the high-stakes question on a game show. He leaned down, kissed her hello, and introduced her to Helen as his cousin Charlotte. He smiled and added, "Or something like that." Charlotte said she had told her husband, Eric, that she could have sworn she saw Christopher arriving at the polo match just as they were leaving.

Over dinner, Eric explained their reason for visiting Bermeja, something about Charlotte's desire to return to a place she remembered from her childhood and Mexico offering promising investment opportunities because of the existence of so many monopolies. Eric never missed a chance to inform those around him that he had made—and was still making—a fortune by running around the world collecting businesses as fast as some people collect friends. When he had heard about the potential sale of a Mexican cell phone company, he had found a reason to grant his wife her wish to return. From what Helen could tell, Eric offered up this last piece of evidence—turning his wife's nostalgia for childhood holidays into an opportunity for acquiring monopolies—as proof of just how clever he was.

As they walked back to Casa Tortuga, Christopher groaned about having agreed to dinner. "Why did you let me do that?"

"Me?"

"Yes, you." He hung his arm over her shoulders.

"Charlotte seems very nice, but does Eric ever not talk about money?"

"I did warn you."

"How exactly are you and Charlotte related?" Christopher's family tree, complicated by too many divorces, remarriages, half and stepsiblings, still confused her.

"My grandmother and Charlotte's mother were married to the same man, but Charlotte's mother was much younger than my grandmother. So technically, she is my step aunt, even though she is only eleven years older."

"So how did they both come to spend time here?"

"You mean my mother and Charlotte's mother?"

"Yes."

"After my grandfather divorced Charlotte's mother, he married again. My grandmother was his first, Charlotte's mother his second. Wife number three was from Venezuela."

"Your grandfather must have been very good-looking and very charming."

"He was. He was also ruthless. I guess Charlotte came here with her mother, which now that I think about it is very odd, because the house belonged to the woman my grandfather left her mother for."

"I thought Charlotte said she used to come here with her father for spring break."

"Oh, well, that might be right. My grandfather. That makes more sense. My mother and my grandfather didn't get along—I think because of the way he treated her mother, so we never spent much time with him. He was never here when we were."

"But Charlotte gave the impression that her family and yours were close."

"That's just Charlotte's way. I didn't meet her until I was just out of law school. We would run across each other from time to time at a party in New York. Her mother was very social, and Charlotte tries hard to be like her."

"Do you have other cousins?"

Christopher put his arm around her waist and pulled her close to answer her question. "I do, yes I do, but I've had too much to drink to remember their names."

There were no lights on the road, but the hard jeweled sky was just bright enough for them to see their way home.

"At least, thank God, Eric and Charlotte are leaving tomorrow. He was very excited to tell me about some bank he was considering buying."

"How could anyone come here and not want to stay forever?"

"Let's just hope they don't like it, because if they do, they'll return on their private planes, their black Denalis with hot and cold running staff will eat up all the roads, they'll invite their friends, most of whom we won't like, and we won't want to come back here because the feeling of just the two of us on this stretch of coast will be gone. Forever. Maybe you should update the article you wrote a year ago, with a sort of World Travel Advisory Warning about it."

"I don't think there is such a thing as a World Travel Advisory Warning."

"There has to be. There should be. Or at least there should be some sort of alert system to avoid encounters with those who are so insufferable about their money."

"He is rather smug. Do you remember his comment that none of the Europeans knew he was in the Forbes 400?"

Christopher stopped for a minute to steady himself. Too much tequila had made him dizzy. "He said that? He really said that?"

She bit her lower lip and nodded. "When he was talking about looking at shooting estates to buy."

"I knew there had to be a reason I was drinking so much."

They resumed the hike. As they reached Casa Tortuga, Christopher shook his head and smiled. "Oh, well, then, we're safe. We have nothing to worry about. Sounds as if Eric is well on his way to stabilizing his status as a social leper without any outside help."

Christopher crashed on their bed and covered his eyes with his hands. Helen lay next to him and rested on her elbows. She reached over and lifted one hand from his eyes. "So, how did you learn to sing so well?"

He turned his head to look at her. "You're assuming I did."

"Charlotte was very clear."

"Ah, the dangers of dinner with Charlotte and Eric persist."

"No, really, please, Christopher. She said you sang at your sister's wedding and that you were really good."

"A long time ago."

"Six years is not that long."

"Okay. If you must know. Five years in a boys' choir at an English boarding school. But you knew that." He enjoyed teasing her precisely because she did not know how to tease back.

"I did. But I didn't know you could still sing. Why haven't you ever sung for me?" She sat up and was shaking his arm. "Come on," she said, laughing. "I want you to sing for me."

He split his fingers apart and looked through them at her.

"First of all, I've had way too much to drink. Second, there are certain things I do only once in my life. And third, . . . I'll think of a third in a minute."

"Why only once? Charlotte said you were good. Seriously good. She said you wore sunglasses and acted a little drunk."

"I probably was."

"So what was the song?"

He shook his head. "I don't remember."

"Of course you do. Come on, Christopher. Please."

"You have found me in a seriously weakened state." He sighed. "Okay, it might have been a Dean Martin song."

"'Moon River'?"

"Great song, but off the grid. Johnny Mercer, not Dean Martin."

"You're sure?"

"Positive."

"'You're Nobody 'Til Somebody Loves You'?"

"Cold."

"'Baby, It's Cold Outside'?"

"Colder."

"That's it. That's all I know. Please, Christopher."

"Okay." He took a deep breath and sighed. "'*Nel Blu Dipinto Di Blu'*—in the blue that is painted blue."

"I don't know it."

"Also known as '*Volare*.'"

"No, really I don't. How does it go?"

"Ahh, clever girl, but not clever enough."

She fell back in defeat next to him. "So you really won't sing for me?"

"No."

"Please." She shook his arm again.

"You do know you have me wrapped around your little finger?"

She kissed him. "Then sing. Please."

"Okay. If I must." He pushed up on his elbow.

"'*Penso che un sogno così non ritorni mai più.*'" He smiled. "It's better in Italian.

"'*Mi dipingevo le mani e la faccia di blu / Poi d'improvviso venivo dal vento rapito / E incominciavo a volare nel cielo infinito.*'"

His voice was muffled in tenderness. It crumbled her heart.

"'*Volare, oh, oh . . . / Cantare, ohohoho . . . / Nel blu dipinto di blu / Felice di stare lassù.*' That's it, that's all I remember."

Helen was quiet as if still listening. "Did you sing it in Italian?"

"I did. It was how my eccentric Italian teacher taught us in our first year. All we did was sing."

"With *sprezzatura*?"

He nodded.

She put her hand on his chest as if to feel for his heart. "Christopher?"

"Yes, my love."

"What is the one thing you will do only once? Only for me. Only once."

"You want to know the one thing that I will do for you that I will not do for anyone else?" He had suddenly become serious.

"Yes, I do. Only for me. Only once."

"Only for you. Only once. Okay, let me think." He looked at her—the heat of the evening had made her long blond hair wispy around her face. "Marry you."

CHAPTER TWELVE

SUSSEX

There are moments when some understanding simultaneously compresses and expands. When Christopher asked Helen to marry him, he surprised himself. He had spent much of his life letting things come to him—waiting—never rushing or trying to force anything. He had come to value, maybe even cherish, a sense of patience—it had almost become a type of religion for him—of letting things play themselves out. Perhaps his ability to see how things would develop or unravel allowed him this equanimity. He understood that events had their own internal sense of motion. Most of his past relationships were two- or three-sentence stories. His ability to see where things were headed was his own form of perfect pitch. It was nothing he had learned—he could never remember not having it. At times he wondered if he had inherited this ability from his father, it certainly wasn't from his mother.

They were married six months later on a beautiful day in June in the village church near Willow Brook. The wedding was small,

Helen's immediate family and neighbors, Christopher's mother, sister, and brother-in-law, a few friends from work and school. Christopher's childhood friend Willie, whom Helen had only met once before, flew over from the States to be the best man. At the beginning of the ceremony, the pastor looked down at Henry, whom Christopher had asked to be the ring bearer, hopping on one foot, and remarked that his church was rarely filled with so much youth and energy and hope.

When Helen walked down the aisle, Christopher thought she had never looked so beautiful. And something about her became clear. Maybe he had always sensed it, but only then did he comprehend it so completely. It was her simplicity surrounded by her ability to live in the present. It wasn't that she tried to look forward and failed, it was more that she never tried. And he had to assume it was because she liked to exist without needing to ask questions about duration or destination. She always seemed happy where she was. She allowed those around her the luxury of not having to plan. It was almost as if it were a gift she bestowed. For as long as he had known her, he had watched as she thought hard about things and then did what she wanted, which generally had more to do with her heart than with any train of logic. And she rarely consulted opinions along the way. It was as if she lived her life by a set of golden rules of improvisation—Don't come in when you're not needed. Listen and be willing to change. Trust. Do not deny or negate. Maybe she did what he admired and could not do. It was her own form of fearlessness. And yet she understood none of the charm she possessed. The idea that there was one thing in the world he could do for her that he had never done for anyone else was something she didn't doubt. She put her trust and faith in possibilities. She made things happen without realizing what she was doing.

As she walked down the aisle, Helen had her own epiphany—if that is even the right word. She observed how little Christopher carried forward from his past. Even his relationship with his sister, Laure—whom she had only just met—seemed distant, respectful, almost formal. Now, as she watched him waiting for her, she would always remember thinking how alone he seemed, as if there were some impenetrable boundary surrounding him. Why did she feel she was on the wrong side?

CHAPTER THIRTEEN

CALA BLAVA

For their honeymoon, Christopher took Helen to a small hotel in Cala Blava on the Majorcan coast. As consolation for the short four-day trip, he planned to take the last four weeks of summer off. Édouard Beaumont had been so pleased with the terms of the sale of his company that he gave them La Mandala for August as a wedding present. Helen had hoped Christopher would consider returning to Bermeja, but he had said it was too far and the summer months too hot and full of rain. She didn't care about distance or heat or rain.

At the outset of the Spanish American War, the Spanish government had expropriated a sizable holding of land from an old Majorcan family and built a small military fort on Majorca's western tip, a wide promontory that pushed out into the Mediterranean Sea. When the government realized there was nothing or no one to defend, they returned the land to the family with the condition that the property remain a nature preserve. After a number of years, the family sold the parcel of land to an architect from Palma who, as a young boy, had sailed many times past the fortress and had dreamed of transforming it into a place to live.

The dirt road through the nature preserve was unlit, but the moon was strong. The land was dry, with stands of scraggly scrub pines. Christopher found the driving difficult because there weren't any signs or markers confirming they were headed in the right direction. After a few miles through land that promised nothing, they saw low lights illuminating the entrance to the hotel. A man dressed in a long white tunic and trousers was waiting. He took their bags and drove them in a golf cart down what once had been a path for goats to a small stone cottage on a piece of land that looked across the water to Africa. It was luxurious and simple—one bedroom and bath, a fireplace, a four-poster bed piled high with a thick white duvet and three rows of crisp white pillows. A small lap pool bordered the edge of the loggia. They were both tired, but Christopher insisted they have the welcome drink that had been left for them—rum with orange peel, cloves, and cinnamon. They sat outside on the terrace. Down below, the hotel's restaurant was serving its last guests. The sound of laughter twisted up toward them.

A steady wind was turning the evening chilly, and Helen went inside to get a shawl.

"So do you feel different?" Christopher asked when she returned.

"No, but I guess I thought I would. That it would feel like some big shift. As if a heavy door had closed behind me. But I don't. It just feels as if everything has become simpler, less complicated."

"I didn't know we had a complicated relationship," he said with a dip of his chin.

"That's not what I mean, it just feels smoother and quieter. How about you?"

"Me? Do I feel different? I don't know. I mean, I never thought that much about getting married, and then when I met you I couldn't imagine ever being without you."

"But what if I had resisted you or played hard to get?"

"I would have had to learn more songs."

They woke up late and Christopher ordered breakfast. A waiter brought a large wicker basket with carafes of hot coffee, tea, and steamed milk, along with breads, fruits, yogurts, and nuts. After a long breakfast, they gathered books and magazines and newspapers.

"What are these?" he asked, pulling several manila folders from the pile.

"Some reading I wanted to do—ideas for my next article."

"Contraband," he said, tossing the folders on top of a suitcase. "If I promised no work, you can, too."

"You're right," she said and put her arms around his neck and kissed him. "What was I possibly thinking?"

An hour later they wandered down to the small cove not far from the hotel. He helped her down the rocks. The water was cold and clear and salty. He proposed a swim to the platform anchored several hundred feet from where they stood. The water was calm, but large swells rolled shoreward in a steady slow rhythm. She stood looking at the water. "It seems pretty far."

"I'll swim alongside. If you get tired, you can hold on to my shoulder."

They started out together, and when she fell behind, he treaded water while she caught up. When they reached the platform, she waited for the dip between the swells to climb the ladder. He followed quickly behind her, climbing the rungs two at a time. They lay on the hot boards with their eyes closed and listened to the dots and dashes of a seagull's cry as it flew over them. The floating platform rocked in slow motion up and over the swells and then down into the troughs. When they had rested, they swam back, the swells pushing them up and forward to the shore. They read until lunch, and later in the afternoon, Christopher repeated the swim. The waves had been building from the morning, and Helen decided not to go. The size of the swells did not faze him. He trusted the sea because it felt familiar. She watched him swim away from her—steady, strong, at ease. When he reached the platform, he turned back. She flipped through a guidebook of the Balearic Islands and read about a monastery located in Valldemossa where Chopin had gone with his lover, George Sand, to recuperate from tuberculosis. The article on the monastery showed an image of a perfectly preserved apothecary from the eighteenth century lined with seventeenth- and eighteenth-century blue-and-white ceramic pots with names of all the drugs and ointments and extracts in Latin. She would have liked to go there, but she knew Christopher would not want to move, so she let the thought drift away as she watched him swim back to her.

Helen was curious to see who would arrive for dinner. At seven P.M., "sunset" cocktails of tequila, pink grapefruit juice, and mint were served on top of the old fort, where Moroccan tents and Persian rugs and comfortable sofas had been arranged. Guests drifted upward—a family of five from England who, from what Helen could tell, were involved in property development; a middle-aged German couple; a group of six—a second marriage with adult children from each side, speaking a mixture of German and French and English; a young Spaniard and his Eastern European girlfriend. Each group stayed to itself. Christopher and Helen remained until shadows stretched into darkness and the seam between the water and sky disappeared.

For four days they followed the same rhythm. They would sleep late and enjoy the wicker baskets of breakfast delivered each morning. They would dress for the beach and bring books and newspapers and walk down the cliff and lie on the rocks. At two they would walk to the restaurant overlooking the sea and share a paella. In the afternoons they played tennis or rode bicycles to the marina. Before dinner, they read in their room or sat on the terrace with a glass of wine. She loved having him all to herself.

On the day they were leaving, they went for one last swim. Several large yachts were headed toward the marina. One pulsed past, brimming with women in bikinis and bare-chested men—all keeping beat to loud club music.

Helen asked Christopher what he thought about an article on the megayachts that were being built for all the Russian oligarchs.

"I told you no discussion of work. I'm surprised you're not the one enforcing this."

"I rather think these waters are neutral territory."

"Okay," he said. "Your logic's not sound, but I'll still answer. No, you shouldn't do it."

"Why?"

"You'll get bored. I've watched you for the past year. In the middle of it, you'll change your mind and decide you don't want to do it. It has no soul."

"Am I that predictable?" she asked as she waded into the water. It was cold. She moved slowly.

"Taking the fifth and changing the subject," he said as he dove in to join her. "Have you ever been to Ibiza?" he asked as he resurfaced.

She chopped water in his direction.

"What's so funny?"

"That there are still questions about each other that we don't know the answer to."

"But why isn't that good?" He combed his hair back with his hands.

"It's neither good nor bad. It's just that I guess I always thought I would know everything about the man I married."

"Mission impossible. So what's the answer?"

"No."

"Really?"

"No, I haven't."

"But I thought it was the party place for all pretty young things from London."

"It is. But I never went."

"No rites of passage?"

"Not for me," she said.

They watched the sun catch the edge of a late afternoon cloud. She shivered and got out of the water. He followed her to the towels they had left on the rocks.

"Now my turn."

"For what?"

"To ask you any question I want."

He laughed.

"It gets worse. You have to answer it."

"Go ahead."

"I'm thinking. Okay, so when you asked me to marry you, did you know you were going to at the time?"

"No."

"No? That's it?"

"I know you think I can always see beyond the next move or the next challenge as if I'm playing chess. And on a lot of things I can and I do. But on some things—"

"Like us?"

"Yes, like us, you're way too unpredictable."

The sun was now completely covered in clouds and the wind was picking up. Helen's teeth chattered and she pulled her towel around her. "Maybe I should have just asked you how many girlfriends you had before me."

"Missed your chance," he said and stood up. He held his hand out to her. "Let's go. It's not going to get any warmer out here."

"You know you're like a matador," she said as he pulled her up.

"How so?"

"You sidestep all my questions."

He shook his head. "Only the ones that don't matter."

Later that night he told her, "I just knew my life could no longer be separate from yours. I knew whatever happened to you would happen to me, too."

Marc picked them up at Heathrow. As he updated Christopher with the latest developments of deals their firm was working on, Helen counted the number of days they had in London before they left in August.

At some point on the drive, Marc turned to Helen and told her he had met a very attractive Italian woman. Her name was Ghislaine and she designed jewelry. She had been married to a much older Italian who had decided one morning he was moving to Costa Rica without her. Marc said Philippe Pavesi had introduced them at the Art Basel fair. Helen recognized the name of his girlfriend as being from an old titled Venetian family, but she did not know if the name were her maiden or married name. Marc was vague about whether she was divorced yet or would even get a divorce, so Helen let him, as she often did, tell her only what he wished her to know—to be the only spinner of the narrative. She was disappointed when Christopher asked Marc to bring Ghislaine to Saint-Tropez in August. She was irritated that he had not discussed it with her first.

CHAPTER FOURTEEN

LONDON

Almost as soon as they returned to London there was an invitation from Fiona Campbell for a girls' lunch. Christopher had been introduced to Fiona and Adrian at a drinks party for Édouard Beaumont earlier in the year. Helen was surprised by the invitation—she had never met Fiona. The Campbells owned the villa down the hill from Édouard, and when Fiona heard they would be taking La Mandala for August, she wanted to meet this young woman of whom Édouard was so enamored.

Helen was expecting not to like Fiona, a former model who, according to Christopher, after she divorced her Australian husband, moved to London to marry a much older and titled Englishman. Christopher told Helen that he would be surprised if she did not like Fiona—she was fun and surprisingly irreverent. Helen was not keen to go, but he pushed her. "You might surprise yourself and have a good time. They are just the type who might know people in Tangier—they might even know Pauling."

David, Helen's editor, had offered her an article on William

Pauling, an Englishman in Morocco who had a rare and controversial piece of Chinese sculpture from the European Pavilions in the Summer Palace. The European Pavilions had been designed by the Jesuit monk Giuseppe Castiglione in the 1700s for the Qianlong Emperor, and the sculpture, also designed by Castiglione, was part of an elaborate clepsydra, which was the centerpiece of the pavilions. The sculpture was the featured piece in Christie's major London sale scheduled for early December and had already received a great deal of attention. The ownership of the sculpture had become an international issue, with China asserting that the statue had been illegally plundered during the Second Opium War and demanding that it be returned.

A massive amount of research was required, and while David did not plan to run the piece until just before the sale, he said there was some urgency. Pauling had agreed to an interview, and David was worried he might change his mind. Pauling had told David he was expecting any journalist David sent to know as much, if not more, about Castiglione than he did. David told Helen to prepare in case Pauling agreed to see her before the start of the summer holidays.

The story was complicated. During the Second Opium War, two British envoys and a journalist met with the Royal Chinese Prince to negotiate a settlement but instead were imprisoned and tortured to death. Lord Elgin, the British High Commissioner to China, retaliated by ordering British and French troops to destroy everything in the Summer Palace, including the European Pavilions. The treasures—porcelains, bronzes, marbles, and jewels—that were not destroyed were plundered by the soldiers. Now the only visual record of the design was a set of twenty engravings executed by the Chinese artist Yi Lantai, who had trained under Castiglione. Castiglione, credited with changing the way Chinese artists viewed perspective, was an intense subject all to himself. With so much research ahead of her, a ladies' lunch in Belgravia did not seem a good use of her time.

When Helen grumbled once more, Christopher reminded her that for all she knew, Adrian might have gone to school with Pauling. "You never know about the connections between these English public school boys." It was enough to push her forward.

Helen was the next to last to arrive. Fiona greeted her with a glass of champagne and introduced her to everyone. She was surprised to meet Marc's girlfriend Ghislaine and wondered if Christopher had known she had been invited. No one seemed to know anyone particularly well. Helen watched Fiona charm everyone; she gave them energy because she had so much herself. The last to arrive was Solange Bolton, an older woman whom Fiona introduced as the wife of Adrian's best friend, Anthony, who had the grandest shooting estate in Northumberland.

Over lunch, Solange admired the looking glass that hung over an early eighteenth-century painted side table and asked if Fiona had just acquired it. "Oh, no, Harry and I had it," she said, referring to her ex-husband. "When Adrian and I moved into this flat, I needed something to hang over that table. I remembered the looking glass Harry and I had. I called him up and asked him for it. He said, 'Fine, darling. I'll have it shipped over to you right away.' Adrian was thrilled. He said it's almost as good as that side table, which he inherited from his grandfather. And that vase," she said, pointing to a Lalique bowl filled with peonies. "I asked Harry if I could have that, too. When we divorced, I must have forgotten to ask for it, but Harry was more than happy to give it to me."

"Sounds as if you've remained good friends," Amanda said. She was tall and blond. Helen suspected that she, too, had once been a model.

"Oh, yes, we've remained very good friends," Fiona said.

"But then why did you divorce?" Amanda asked.

"He had a little girl on the side, and when I asked him if he was going to give her up, he said no. Harry has to be the most generous man on the planet, not a mean bone in his body, but he has a weakness for little tarts, and I would not tolerate it, so that's why we divorced. But nothing much has changed. We still talk on the telephone once a week, and when he comes to London, we always have dinner."

Amanda was surprised. She was getting divorced. She had a four-year-old son about whom she was concerned. When Ghislaine asked her if she was certain it was over, she said yes, that really they should never have gotten married. "He was so good-looking, and I was determined to beat my best friend down the aisle." Amanda said this last statement half seriously. "You know, Richard has never grown up. Except for the first year of our marriage, I suspect he has always had a girlfriend."

"How did you know?" Helen asked.

"Oh, lots of ways. The last time it was his tie. By then I had just had enough."

"What do you mean?" Ghislaine asked.

Amanda explained. "Richard's always been terribly snobby about his ties. It has to be either Turnbull and Asser or Hermès. We were on our way to a dinner party, and he had on this hideous tie. He asked me, 'So what do you think of my tie?' as if he were trying to bait me. And I said, 'I think it's hideous.' 'You don't like it?' he asked me. 'No, I don't,' I said. 'Where did you get it?' 'I just saw it in the Next sale.' 'When did you go into Next?' 'Oh, I don't remember, it was in the window, and I was walking by, and I saw it and liked it.'" Amanda spoke in a way to imitate his hurried tone, which was meant to put an end to the discussion of the tie.

"And then when we got to the dinner party, he announced, 'Amanda doesn't like my tie.' I just couldn't figure out what was going on, so the next day I drove up to the Next shop in Cheltenham and asked the shop girl about the striped tie that was in the sale. She didn't know what I was talking about, so I said, 'You know, the smart stripy one that is red and green.' And then she said, 'Oh. I know which one you mean. It's not in the sale, it's never been in the sale, it's upstairs.' And then you just start checking. When they leave early in the morning and they aren't at work, or when they come home late. At Ascot last year I went up to his best friend and asked, 'Jonathan, you have to tell me, is it still going on?' and he just bit his lower lip and nodded his head."

"I know what that's like," Ghislaine broke in. "I was emptying the pockets of my husband's suit and I found a note. He had been traveling quite often to Costa Rica. One of his best friends had gone there to check on some sugar plantations he had inherited. He invited Giovanni to go with him. I didn't go because I was in the middle of redecorating all the rooms of his family's villa outside of Lucca. When Giovanni brought me there as a bride, the place hadn't been touched for almost a century. I told him there was no way we were going to invite people to come stay with us for the weekend unless all the bedrooms were redone. So I set out straightaway getting the place sorted. Anyway, I didn't go to Costa Rica. And after Giovanni arrived, he called me and said he was going to stay a few more weeks, did I mind? He came home and then went back to Costa Rica a few months later. He had some feeble excuse as to why I shouldn't go. And I guess I should have been suspicious then, but I think I was too caught up in everything I was doing at home.

"This time Giovanni stayed six months, and when he returned, I unpacked his bags and found a note from this woman. It turns out he had been having an affair with her the entire time he was there. After we divorced, he moved to Costa Rica, but he left her a few months later. I never knew what she looked like, but I've been told that she was very beautiful. Very Latin looking. From a fairly nice family. I've always wondered if she knew Giovanni was married. After Giovanni left her, he married a girl he had known for only a few months. And now I hear he's left her and taken up with a portrait painter who had come to stay with them in Lucca." Ghislaine's openness and her unadorned tone about being so badly treated drew everyone to her. Helen would later wonder if that had been the point.

Solange, who had been listening to all this, said she would never leave her husband. She was certain he'd had affairs. "It is the way of the man," she said and poked her head forward and turned the corners of her mouth down.

"I would kill my husband if he had an affair," Helen said.

Solange looked at Helen, sizing her up before speaking. "But of course you feel that way," she said. "You are young and in love. A marriage goes through many stages."

Fiona switched the subject by asking Solange about their estate. Was it true that they were selling Eastthorpe to some rich Americans?

"It's not all tragedy. They will give it a much-needed restoration. I can't tell you the number of leaks in the roof. Anthony's family has been patching it for years. It is hard to see it go, but at least Anthony hasn't turned it into a conference center. They never work. The truth is—it needs new stewardship, and why not a rich American? You know it was hard at first for Anthony, but now it has become strangely liberating."

As the women left Fiona's, Solange invited Helen to come have a glass of sherry. She lived a few blocks away. Helen explained that she had to get back to work.

"Ah, why am I not surprised. You are quiet and you observe."

Helen laughed. "Maybe, but I couldn't match any of those stories. When Amanda asked me if I had ever shoplifted . . ."

"Bored, silly young women. Maybe they are the ones who should take lovers. I will walk with you to the corner. What do you write?"

When she told Solange about her next article, Solange reached into her handbag and gave her a card. "I know exactly who he is. He bought my family's house outside of Tangier. You see—I know all about letting go. Call me tomorrow with the dates of your travel, and I will write to him."

CHAPTER FIFTEEN

LONDON

"Odd but interesting" was the way Helen described the lunch to Christopher when he returned home from work that evening. "You know who was there? Ghislaine. You didn't tell me she was a friend of Fiona's."

"News to me. I wonder how they became friends."

"I didn't get a chance to ask her. Almost everyone had some sort of confession about her husband's infidelity. Including Ghislaine."

"Really?" Christopher batted back the conversation. His mind was elsewhere. He didn't like gossip.

"Ghislaine was surprisingly open. I can see why Marc appeals so much to her. Apparently her first husband started having an affair within months of their marriage."

Christopher could feel Helen getting irritated with him. But he was troubled by some of the developments at work. Over the past year, Marc had begun acting as a trading agent for large blocks of shares. For a small firm with limited capital, such business could produce a windfall, but it wasn't business that could be counted on. As long as they remained small, with low overhead, and only acted as agent, there was very little downside to the firm's financial stability and success. Christopher had reviewed the year-to-date results with Marc. The trading profits, which had increased steadily each month, seemed almost too good, and Christopher had questioned him. He had not liked how defensive and arrogant Marc had become.

"Have you had dinner?"

"No, I was waiting for you."

"Want to walk to Oliveto?"

"Sure. Oh, and I forgot to mention the most important thing. Have you ever run across Solange Bolton?"

"No, but if she's married to Anthony Bolton, then I know who you mean."

"She is. She was at Fiona's."

"I was invited to a shoot at their estate in Norfolk last year—Eastthorpe. It's well known. I didn't go. Why?"

"She told Fiona they were selling it to quote 'a rich American who has made all his money in less than a decade. He is very short, but his wife is very nice.' You don't think it could be Eric and Charlotte, do you?"

"Who knows, could be. They certainly are rich enough. It's just the type of place Eric would want to own. Didn't he tell us in Mexico he had been looking for one?"

"That's why I thought it might be him. You'll never believe this, or maybe you will. Solange knows William Pauling, turns out he bought her family's villa outside of Tangier. She said she would write to him. When do you want to say, 'I told you so'?"

"Never. By the way, Marc and I have to go to Milan next week, so I'll miss the art opening Ghislaine invited us to, but Marc said Ghislaine is still planning to go. He said she'll swing by and pick you up."

When they returned home from dinner, Christopher stayed up to review documents his office had sent him.

CHAPTER SIXTEEN

LONDON

A week later, Ghislaine arrived in a chauffeur-driven Mercedes. Helen noticed that she was dressed in the latest summer style—a flippy pink-and-green floral printed skirt, pale pink cashmere twin set, pale green mules. Ghislaine told her that the *Evening Standard* had picked up the opening and was sending a photographer. Helen wondered how she knew this. The driver dropped them off in front of the gallery. People had spilled out from the entrance. Almost everyone was dressed in black, and many were drinking or smoking or both. Inside, a well-known, aged rock star stood in the middle of the room speaking to the gallery owner and the featured artist. A middle-aged man came up and introduced himself to Helen and Ghislaine. He was disappointed they did not recognize him.

"You must not be familiar with this artist's work, because if you were, you would know that I am the pink rabbit." He spoke with a heavy French accent and focused more on Helen than Ghislaine, whose eyes were flitting and flicking around the room.

"The pink rabbit?" Helen asked.

"Yes, the pink rabbit."

"I don't understand." She turned to Ghislaine. "Do you understand?"

He answered for her. "He"—the man threw his chin toward the artist, who was still standing in the center of the gallery—"did a series of paintings of a dealer as the pink rabbit. I am the pink rabbit. It's making you see the dealer in a way that he is not. To me that is what new art is all about. Making new relationships, making the familiar look unfamiliar, and he has a lot of humor. Here is the dealer"—he patted his chest—"someone who should be serious—he gives advice—accepts or rejects artists—sells pictures worth millions and millions. But if he is a pink rabbit, well, then, you can't take him too seriously, can you? And then he did an exhibition called *The Girl or the Pink Life*."

"I'm not sure I understand. What is the pink life?" Helen found his use of pronouns confusing.

"Haven't you heard of Edith Piaf?" he asked. "*C'est incroyable.*"

"Edith Piaf, of course. I just don't understand what the pink life is."

"La vie en rose."

"We would say the rosy life."

The owner of the gallery quieted everyone to introduce the artist—"Popular, unpopular, hard, soft, classic, new"—and then he raised a glass of champagne and everyone clapped. Helen leaned toward Ghislaine and asked her if she understood what he was saying. Ghislaine shook her head but kept clapping. The gallery owner came over and kissed Ghislaine and introduced himself to Helen. He invited them to a light supper at his house after the opening. He told Ghislaine that his office had received Marc's offer and would respond by the end of the week. When he walked away, Ghislaine, elated they had received a personal invitation to the supper, offered more than she might otherwise have. She told Helen that Marc had made an offer on a Jim Dine dressing gown. "He only did four, and Marc said Dine hasn't moved up like some of the others. He thinks it would look great on the wall. It would really be a statement."

On the drive to the gallery owner's house, Ghislaine said it was plain and surprisingly drab. "His wife not only has no taste, she has no style." Helen had begun to notice that Ghislaine could finish people off with bold declarative statements. On arrival, Helen was taken aback to hear Ghislaine tell the woman who opened the door that her house was her favorite in London.

"I love how understated it is. So chic," she said, adding that she hoped she could get her help when she and Marc eventually bought a house.

So this is how she operates, Helen thought, and she began to look backward at many of the statements Ghislaine had made.

CHAPTER SEVENTEEN

SAINT-TROPEZ

They flew into Nice at the beginning of August. Helen had convinced Christopher to rent a car so they could drive along the coast to Saint-Tropez. He had wanted to take a helicopter and have a car delivered. He and Marc judged things not by how much they cost but how much time they took. What should have been an hour-and-a-half car drive took four hours, and Christopher was irritated, more impatient than she had ever seen him. When it started to rain, she thought of their being in a slow mudslide of cars, but she dared not share the image with him because she was fearful his irritation would thicken into anger.

His impatience evaporated once they passed through the gates of the private enclave where La Mandala was located. They ascended as they had with Édouard—zigzagging back and forth on a road lined with tall cypress trees. Danny, the Irish house manager, was waiting for them. La Mandala appeared larger without Édouard. All the bedrooms had names; theirs was called Isola Bella because of the hand-blocked wallpaper of a garden and views through French doors of the Mediterranean Sea. The bed, sofa, and chaise were all upholstered in a pale blue silk chosen to match the color of the sky.

On the peak next to La Mandala was the citadel, the medieval fortress, hexagonal in shape, with walls two feet thick. Below the citadel was the town cemetery. The nightclubbers, who journeyed to Saint-Tropez in the dark hours of night and left just before sunrise, parked their cars along the cemetery wall.

Saint-Tropez hadn't changed much since the seventeenth century—narrow streets lined with two-story buildings stuccoed in sunbaked colors. The only things that ever fluctuated were the line of the sea and the crowd of tourists who descended upon the quaint harbor town suddenly in June like a net of birds and left just as suddenly at the end of August.

In the morning they would stand on the terrace and watch boats racing away, and in the evening they would watch the same boats racing back. Parallel lines of white all pointing toward the horizon. They could have spent all day on the terrace of La Mandala without ever having to leave. Perhaps it was curiosity or the feeling of missing something or just the desire for change that would cause them to leave the grounds. Or maybe it was all just a little too perfect. Every afternoon of the first week, Christopher and Helen would walk down the steep hill and follow the shoreline into town, and Christopher would buy all the English papers and a *Herald Tribune,* and they would sit at a café and order citron pressés or sometimes espressos to fortify themselves for the walk back.

Friends came and went during August. Some came for lunch and some came for dinner, others for long weekends. When Helen looked back on that summer, she realized that in the first year of their marriage, Christopher was always adding people, and she was always taking them away.

A table had been placed on the east side of the house overlooking the bay of Saint-Tropez. Large teak dining chairs with pale, stone-colored cushions stood at attention. For breakfast, large jewel-colored carafes of coffee and fresh orange juice arrived, followed by fresh bread and croissants and pains au chocolat. Guests would slowly meander to the table. Helen always arrived first in those quiet early mornings. The sun had not risen enough to have full strength. There was always a stillness in those mornings that made Helen think the earth had paused in its slow orbit. Lunches of melons and prosciutto, grilled fish, and crudités served on pieces of cork bark were served at one.

After lunch, everyone drifted to the pool with books and magazines. Later, guests would wander into town to pick up a newspaper, or window-shop, or have a drink at one of the bars in the port and watch the parade of people and boats. Le Gorille was the oldest café and had the best seats. Its black-and-blue-striped awning reached deep into the crowd. People sat down at the cafés as if they were taking their seat at the theater. As a yacht edged around the concrete wall of the harbor, makeup would be freshly applied, windblown hair swept back, poses assumed, as if a curtain were about to rise. Athletic young men in white polo shirts with the names of the boats on their pockets adjusted towels and mats with the owners' insignias. The names always reminded Helen of racehorses on fourth-rate tracks—Lucky Lady, Lovely Lassie, Pretty Woman, Fortune's Girl.

In the late afternoon, Christopher and Helen would lie on their bed and read before dinner. Sometimes she felt as if they were between acts in a play. She lost him during the day, but in the evening he would return to her. As if everything were reset. She could always find him at night.

On many evenings the table was set for twelve. Friends and acquaintances who spent August in the South of France would come for dinner and finally leave in the early hours of the morning—several hours later than they had planned, because there was something about La Mandala that made everyone feel as if they were meant to stay. After dinner, they would meander over to the terrace in front of the house and talk against the candlelight. It was quiet except for the sounds of the Byblos disco, which pulsed from the town below. Guests would stay until the river of cars that snaked into Sainte-Maxime had disappeared.

Many people came and went that August, but the one Helen would remember was Willie, who was the best man at their wedding. After university, Willie had early success as a playwright for a triptych of plays about a decadent, decaying Scottish family. Hailed by the *Evening Standard* as an original voice, he had surprised none of his close friends when he had not followed with others. His three plays were about his family. He had run out of material. He settled into a position teaching playwriting and acting at a university in England, and then, a number of years later, was offered a visiting professorship at a small university in New York City. A year later, he was surprised to be offered a permanent position. He was even more surprised when he accepted.

Christopher was pleased that Willie and Helen got along so well. In the evenings, he would often seat them next to each other, and she would ask him about his work. Willie told her stories about Christopher and himself. Christopher was one of the cool boys, clever at school and good at sport—even the bullies behaved better when he was around. "I would never have passed my O levels in maths if it had not been for him. In fact, I think he tutored half the boys in our house in maths. I'm not surprised he ended up in finance, he always seemed to find a sense of peace and order in numbers. And he always had a sixth sense for when one of the boys in our house was going to get in trouble and managed to steer him toward safety and cover. Some of the boys, including me, had some pretty dysfunctional families and didn't have anyone looking out for them. I, for one"—and Willie said raising his hand—"could have been kicked out at least twice had it not been for Christopher. He'll make a good father."

After five days, Willie began to consider the sun. He couldn't understand its position. Looking across the harbor at the Mediterranean, the sun rose on the right. Why did the sun seem to rise in the west and set in the east? Optical illusion? Saint-Tropez must face north? Various theories were floated. "Maybe we have been wrong all these years," Willie said. He let his words drift into the air like lazy smoke. He smiled and confirmed his judgment. "Yes, we have—it's all so simple now." He liked to think that such luxurious living could overturn the world of science. They argued about it again at lunch. Willie organized a mock expedition into town to buy a map to settle the question once and for all.

CHAPTER EIGHTEEN

SAINT-TROPEZ

At the end of the second week, Marc arrived with Ghislaine. Within an hour of their appearance, Ghislaine, who had never been to Saint-Tropez, asked Helen to take her on a tour of the town. Marc stayed behind to discuss a few business matters with Christopher. Helen and Ghislaine walked down Avenue Paul Signac, and when they passed the painter's house, Helen told her about the musée de l'Annonciade with rooms devoted to Signac, Vuillard, Bonnard, and Denis. She assumed Ghislaine would be delighted to go, but she only wanted to shop. She had Marc's credit card and she needed to find a dress for dinner. The small boutiques with summery Provençal clothes were of no interest to her. She asked about a shop a girlfriend had mentioned. While she was trying on dresses, Helen wandered down to the port and bought a collection of newspapers. She returned to find Ghislaine with a pile of clothes at the cash register. She told Helen they would have to take a taxi back because the bags would be too heavy.

When Christopher asked Helen how the afternoon went, she

said how different women looked once you got to know them. He didn't follow up, and she could tell he didn't want her to have a negative view of Marc's girlfriend. She didn't tell him that when she had asked Ghislaine about her jewelry designs, she had said she didn't design jewelry. The next day, Ghislaine left in the late morning to meet a friend for lunch at Club 55 and did not return until late afternoon.

The day before Marc and Ghislaine left, Danny, the house manager, came out to the pool and told Christopher there was a phone call for Marc. A wealthy Asian entrepreneur, Anthony Wu, was calling Marc about selling his block of shares in a large media company. Mr. Wu did not want to speak on cell phones. Danny returned with a phone that he plugged into a jack in the pool cabana. Willie, who was struggling with a book on the postmodern theater, put it down to listen to the conversation.

Marc told Anthony he had to make a few phone calls. He would call him back.

Everyone watched as Marc called a trader and laid out the opportunities and risks of the transaction. A pause. "Fifty thousand shares at six twenty-nine. Okay." He clicked the phone off.

After he had calculated the sum to be in excess of three hundred million pounds, Willie asked Marc, "Were you just working?"

"Yes. A wealthy Chinese entrepreneur just asked us to buy his block of shares. I called a trading partner at Credit Suisse and asked if he wanted to buy the block, and he said he'd get back to me on price."

"The whole amount?"

"The whole block."

To all who watched, it was obvious Marc had done this kind of trade many times before. He knew he had about thirty minutes before the trading partner would call back.

He put the phone down and jumped in the pool.

Willie had now disengaged himself from his reclining position and was sitting with his feet over the side, elbows bent, with his hands on his knees.

"But what if you miss the call?"

"They'll call back." Marc slapped the air with the back of his hand.

Willie resumed his recline but did not return to his book. Helen saw that Willie couldn't accept that this was the way business was conducted, that it was, in fact, much simpler than he had imagined.

The telephone rang just about the time Marc was getting out of the pool and drying himself off.

"Hello," he said. "Okay, fine." He tapped another telephone number.

"Anthony. Fine, they'll do the deal at six twenty-nine. For all fifty thousand shares. Okay. Fine. You're done." Marc began punching in another number.

Willie asked Christopher what was happening. Christopher smiled and held up a finger to indicate that the answer would come from Marc's conversation.

"Philippe, agreed. Six twenty-nine, all fifty thousand shares. Your show now," Marc said.

As they were getting dressed for dinner, Helen brought up the subject of Marc's poolside trade. She thought he was showing off in front of Ghislaine, but Christopher defended him. "I wouldn't make too much of it. Of course he did it for effect, but more for amusement than anything else. And Willie was clearly enjoying the spectacle."

"When did you start dealing with Credit Suisse? I thought you always dealt with Morgan Stanley?"

"Philippe Pavesi works for Credit Suisse."

"Are you and Marc trading?"

"No, just acting as agents—not principals—on selected deals—"

"You can do that?"

"Marc has a brokerage license in Italy."

"Why would someone go through your firm and not deal directly?"

"Trust and anonymity."

"But if it's really true about his father being kicked out of Italy for financial scandal, does it make sense for you and Marc to be associated with Philippe?"

Christopher put his arms around her and kissed the back of her neck. "You say the most romantic things to me."

"Christopher, I'm being serious."

"I know you are."

"Please take me seriously."

"I do, I will. Look, neither you nor I know the real story. All we know is gossip. So I don't think it's fair to conflate Philippe with his father." He looked at her and questioned her assumptions without saying anything. "I wouldn't worry about Marc," he said buttoning his shirt. "He always lands on his feet."

Helen knew that while Christopher always believed the best of someone, he never stopped being vigilant for contradictions, for any signs at variance with the way the person wished to be seen. But with Marc, he seemed to have stopped paying attention.

During dinner, the phone rang and Marc stepped inside to take the call. A few minutes later, he returned to the table. "Hey, Willie, you know that trade—we just made six million quid."

"You just did?"

"No, I mean we all did, everyone who was involved in the trade."

Marc and Ghislaine left the next day on a boat Philippe Pavesi had sent for them. He was meeting them at the Monte-Carlo Beach Hotel to celebrate.

Every Tuesday and Friday morning in August, vendors set up stands in the town square and sold everything from pistachio nuts to antique lace. Helen wove her way through the jumble of stalls shaded by geometric rows of old sycamore trees. The scents of the market—cheeses, roasted meats, spices, lavender—all tangled together in the heat and dust of the day. She stopped to watch a man selling chameleons cut from green-and-orange-striped Styrofoam and fastened to the end of a straightened wire coat hanger. He made the chameleon twist one way and then another to the delight of a little boy. She thought of Henry and Leonora. "*Combien*?" Helen asked. "*Deux euros, et pour deux, trois euros,*" he said. She handed him the coins and took the chameleons and let them dance for her all the way up the hill to La Mandala.

Christopher and Willie had gone exploring. Willie had spent several weeks one summer with his aunt and uncle at a villa in Saint-Tropez. Armed with nothing more than childhood memories, he and Christopher had made a plan to look for the villa. They returned with news that the villa was found, or at least Willie announced it would "do." But the gate was closed and a large German shepherd prowled the grounds. Willie had tried unsuccessfully to convince Christopher that the sign *Cave Canem* meant Ignore the Canine.

One afternoon when they were lying together in their bedroom, Helen told Christopher what Willie had said about how he would be a good father. "Do you ever think about that? About having kids?"

"Sure, don't you?"

"Why have you never brought it up?"

"I don't know, I guess because it depends on you, what you want. And both of us have been working long hours, I've been traveling a lot, it just doesn't seem the best time now. When I don't have to travel so much, it'll be better. But how do you feel?"

"I know, you're right. Maybe I'm just anxious you're never going to slow down."

"I understand. I will, though. But for now, the show must go on—at least for a bit longer."

When Helen learned that her friend Peregrine had not organized any summer holiday plans, partly because his work was not going well but mostly for financial reasons, she sent him a ticket. The day he arrived, he pronounced himself Captain of Games. All the guests were lying around the pool, napping or reading crinkled newspapers or copies of water-waffled magazines, when Peregrine made his announcement: a backgammon tournament would take place the following day. Willie looked up, raised his hand, and offered to be in charge of house colors. Everyone was required to play. Peregrine, who often gave his friends titles because he thought they either deserved them or coveted them, revivified an extinct dukedom and conferred it on Willie, immediately addressing him as "Your Grace," which delighted Willie.

Christopher was surprised Helen did not know how to play. He would teach her. He set up the board and explained the rules. He was good at games. On each roll of the dice, he showed her the choices—the risky move and the safe move—because he knew she didn't have any instinct for strategy. He would look up and ask her if she understood what he was doing.

On the following day, she walked to the pool and found Christopher and Peregrine playing the finals. Christopher shook the dice in his cupped hands and rolled. He watched the pieces—it was almost as if by intensity and concentration he could will them where he wanted them to go. When he shook the dice, he had already calculated what he needed to move ahead. He would take chances, and when they went against him, he didn't react, he just concentrated harder and watched with more intensity. Just as Christopher was about to win, fat raindrops fell on the board. A rain delay was declared and a draw was agreed.

A few days before Willie left, he, Peregrine, and Helen walked into town to an art and antique fair she had seen advertised on a poster. Large canvas tents had been set up on the far side of the port. They paid the admission fee and walked down the aisles, looking carefully at what each dealer had to offer. Willie veered off to find the displays of the local artists, and Helen and Peregrine continued down the aisle of stalls selling china and jewelry and small pieces of furniture. As she was looking at a set of dessert knives and forks with cloisonné handles, Peregrine disappeared and then reappeared in a pea-green coat lined with fur.

"Look what I found. There're great vintage clothes over there," he said pointing behind him.

"Peregrine, it's dreadful. Looks like someone has died."

"I'm quite certain someone did. Why else would this be here? I reckon," he said, "it dates to the nineteen thirties. Look how well made it is." He held his arm out to show her the cuff. "I think it's French. It's very warm."

She started to laugh. "Take it off. It's awful."

"Really? It's bloody good value," he said. "Look, it's real fur." The stall keeper had come to find him. "*Je vais envisager de l'acheter,*" Peregrine said, taking off the coat and handing it back.

Helen, who was still laughing, shook her head. They found Willie, who was buying a small pencil drawing of three palm trees clustered on a point of land.

The evening before Willie left, Fiona and Adrian asked Christopher and Helen and all their guests down for drinks and a light dinner. Fiona had prepared a delicious supper of salad and lobster thermidor. Adrian served a rosé from a cousin's vineyard. *They had a nice life,* Helen thought. They both took care of each other in their own way. Adrian gave Fiona financial security and social standing, and she loved planning and organizing his social gatherings and, as he pointed out, laughed at all his jokes. But Helen thought no one would ever accuse them of being in love. She doubted that they had ever raised their voices at one another.

After dinner, Adrian insisted everyone stay for another drink. Willie excused himself—he was leaving early the next morning. Helen asked him to wait, she would go back with him. On the walk back up the hill, Willie began to invent new constellations. "Look over there. Without a question that has to be Samuel Beckett's forehead. I saw George Bernard Shaw's beard just the other night, and I've been told on very clear nights, such as this one, Marilyn Monroe's lips can be seen in the northwest quadrant." When Helen began to laugh, he said to her, "It's all true. Really it is." And then he said, "I'm going to miss you. I'm going to miss our talks at dinner. I'm going to miss a lot about you."

He waited for her to say something. And when she didn't, he took a step back.

The next morning, she drove him to the heliport. The air was cool, and she felt the end of summer with each deep breath she took. He kissed her good-bye, got out of her car, and then leaned back in. "Keep an eye on Christopher. He assumes everyone has his best interests at heart. Not all of us are so pure."

When she returned to the house, she walked to the front terrace and watched the seagulls find their own levels and drift across the sky. She listened for the sound of children's voices from the beach below.

CHAPTER NINETEEN

LONDON

While Marc was in Saint-Tropez, he had spoken to Christopher about getting larger space for their firm. With several high-profile successes, they had gained respect from the financial establishment in England. They had grown faster than they had anticipated, and Marc wanted to expand the trading and asset management businesses. He had followed his transaction for Anthony Wu with similar transactions for a few select clients, and young, successful entrepreneurs were beginning to come to him for investment advice.

About the agency business, he was so full of conviction that Christopher did not try to oppose him. What worried Christopher was not the agency business, but Marc crossing over into proprietary trading. Given the size of their firm, one bad trade could wipe them out. It exposed them to a great deal of risk, and they did not have much of a capital base to support it. But Christopher knew that people like Marc did whatever they wanted, no matter the opposition. At the best investment firms, competence and independence were correlated. He would have to watch Marc—that's all there was to it.

They did not renew their lease on Birdcage Walk and instead found new office space in the City on Blackfriars Lane, a small street off Fleet Street. Helen liked the address, which was a block from Saint Paul's Cathedral. She informed Christopher that the Black Friars were a Dominican order who wore black hooded capes over their white robes. Within the year, Marc had set up a small trading arm in Milan and traveled back and forth between London and the new location.

As their business grew, Christopher continued to manage the advisory business, and he began to look at opportunities in private equity. He was well suited for both businesses; he was good at listening, and Europeans liked the young half-French, half-American, who, unlike his counterparts at large American banks, was not brash and yet every bit as smart and analytical. He was disciplined and rational—the romance of a vision or belief in what a business might become never slanted his judgment. The young associates in his firm liked working with him because he gave them a great deal of freedom and scope to find investment opportunities and allowed them to present them at the investment committee meeting each Monday morning. And in those meetings Christopher was never sarcastic or abrasive. His voice, in fact, was so uninflected that it almost seemed as if he were uninterested, and yet he could ask the one question that exposed multiple flaws in an associate's proposal.

When they returned from Saint-Tropez, Christopher talked to Helen about looking at houses. Their mews house would be too small if they had children. Most of the time, she went on her own. If she liked anything, she would make a second appointment for Christopher to come back with her. As she went on these house tours, they began to bother her. She found herself unable to stop analyzing the houses to guess who lived in them. Houses were like shells—the shapes of which defined their inhabitants, and rooms like fingerprints that identified a marriage. She had a theory that if the master bedroom was the room that had the most attention to detail, then it was the home of two people who loved each other. If the drawing room and dining room were the rooms most cared for, then the couple were more focused on their social life and less on themselves. Sometimes she thought about how she would analyze their mews house. What, if anything, would it reveal was missing from the life she shared with Christopher?

The house she liked the most had a small conservatory with lemon and lime trees. It had a book-lined dining room and the master bedroom was painted a soft blue gray. It was owned by a developer whose artist wife had decorated it for themselves, but her husband had decided to sell it. Helen was in love with it and she called Christopher almost immediately, but when he came to see it, he saw where the ceiling had been painted recently and he suspected a bad water leak. He thought the developer was asking too much. Christopher made an offer, but it was too low, and the house was sold to someone else. The estate agent called Helen to tell her the bad news. On hearing her disappointment, the estate agent wanted to know what sort of place Christopher had lived in before they were married, and Helen could not answer. Christopher's indifference to where and how they lived eroded her sense of hope. She began to feel that her enthusiasm for looking at houses was a manufactured one that had no basis.

After that summer in Saint-Tropez, they had dinner only once with Marc and Ghislaine, to celebrate the opening of the new office. Christopher had felt the chill between the two women. He figured it had something to do with Ghislaine only being interested in women who could help her get where she wanted to be. He also knew—he had seen it before—the way Helen reacted to women like Ghislaine. Their system of values—power and social status always trumping love—offended her. She would retreat into a position of observation that had a hint of disdain about it. But it was Marc, not Ghislaine, who was bothered by her attitude—Ghislaine was too much of a survivor to notice subtleties or slights. Helen didn't allow Marc, who was from Rochester but who wanted everyone to believe he was from Rome, enough room to recalibrate and re-create himself. When she complained and criticized Marc, Christopher told her that she was underestimating what it was like to be on the outside of something. She had never experienced it, and even though she could try to imagine it, unless she had felt it, she would never understand.

Marc and Ghislaine slipped away one weekend and were married in Rome. Christopher told Helen that Ghislaine was four months pregnant. Helen was surprised they had not been invited, and she said something to Christopher.

"Why? Would you have wanted to go? I thought you didn't particularly like either one of them." She was annoyed by how his cold rationality overrode any objection to disloyalty.

"I still think you—we—should have been invited."

"He said it was just family and close friends in Rome."

A few weeks later, Helen was assigned to write a short piece on the items Christie's regarded as the highlights of the upcoming auctions. As she was leaving the St. James showrooms, she ran into Ghislaine, who explained that she was going to view *The Collection of a Roman Nobleman*. Marc had given her a flat in Milan as a wedding gift and she needed to find one or two important pieces for it. Helen sensed that Ghislaine was becoming one of those women whose ability to acquire expensive objects created a sense of superiority.

"Did you know they bought a flat in Milan?"

"Marc said he was looking for something as an investment."

"Ghislaine was shopping for furniture at Christie's."

Christopher shrugged. "Marc is in the Milan office quite a bit. Maybe Ghislaine wants to live there." He didn't say anything more, even though he knew she wanted him to, but he did think to himself that he should check on the Milan office. He was scheduled to fly to Hong Kong to meet with the founder of an up-and-coming private company who wanted to speak to him about finding European investors. He decided to fly to Milan on the way back to see for himself what was going on.

Solange Bolton wrote Helen with news that William Pauling had agreed to see her. He did not have a computer and only corresponded by post. She should write to him and suggest a date, and he would write back to confirm. She suggested if Helen had time, she should bring her husband and take a tour of the desert. But if they only had a few days they should go to the charming Riad Madani in Marrakech, which had once been the home of Grand Vizier El Glaoui. The idea of a weekend with Christopher at a small hotel in an exotic location thrilled Helen. She hoped they might have time to take a guide into the desert. Christopher might be exhausted and prefer to relax around the pool. She didn't care what they did as long as they were together.

CHAPTER TWENTY

TANGIER

The week before Helen was scheduled to interview William Pauling, the controversy about the statue was resolved privately with both sides committing not to speak about the agreement. Without quotes from the Chinese officials or William Pauling or the auction house, an article on the controversy would be too weak. David still wanted her to write a profile of Pauling—he was an interesting man—but he cut the article to a quarter of the original size. The third son of an earl, an aging aesthete who had spent his life in Tangier, an impresario of sorts, Helen felt it was all well-trodden ground. And it was. The only thing that interested her about him now was his response to her formal letter asking for an interview. He sent her letter back with a weary "Come" sprawled diagonally across the sheet of paper. His gesture revealed his sense of superiority in the world of manners. A few days later a postcard arrived with the typed address and time she should arrive.

Helen checked with her doctor about travel to Morocco. He recommended the hepatitis A vaccine as a precaution and warned her about contaminated water. She told her doctor that Christopher was planning to join her for a few days. He would be coming from Asia, and she doubted they would do much more than relax around the pool at the hotel. Her doctor said Christopher would be well advised to get the vaccine, too.

The day Christopher left for Hong Kong, he received a breathless call from Charlotte announcing that she and Eric had bought Eastthorpe. It was, according to her, in dire need of everything new, but they were having one house party in December before the restoration began the following year, a "bon voyage" to the past, and Charlotte had called Christopher first. She wanted to make certain her "favorite cousin and his charming wife" could come before she set the date. Christopher understood that Charlotte had phrased the invitation in such a way as to give him little choice. He assumed Eric would invite as many successful businessmen as possible. It would be smart for him to attend, though it was not something he was looking forward to. But he knew it was always best to meet future clients in settings unrelated to business, where neither party needed or wanted anything.

When he landed in Hong Kong, Christopher went straight to his meeting. The situation in Hong Kong was promising—a start-up Chinese company that only sold white shirts on the internet. In China, white shirts were the uniforms for work all over the country, and demand for cheap, easily obtainable white shirts offered this company huge growth potential. But it was complicated as to what percentage of ownership a foreigner could hold and how limited the exit strategy could be. Meetings with legal and financial advisors were extended into the coming days because Christopher knew that if he didn't get an agreement hammered out while he was there, it would never happen. Without someone managing every step, smoothing out every wrinkle and roadblock, the transaction would stall and the deal would fall apart. He would have to tell Helen he would not be able to join her in Marrakech.

Several days before she was scheduled to leave, Helen felt odd. She wondered if she were having a reaction to the vaccine. The feeling of a buzz in her body did not go away, and she went to see her doctor. He suspected she might be pregnant. He did an ultrasound and showed her the small sac with a beating heart. She was nine weeks pregnant. She asked if the vaccine he had given her could be a problem. He told her there was very little information, but the hep A vaccine wasn't a live virus and so highly, highly unlikely to be a worry. She couldn't wait to tell Christopher. She knew it was early days, but she felt light-headed with happiness.

When he reached her the following day, he sounded exhausted and said he was extending his stay in Hong Kong. He wouldn't be able to meet her in Morocco. She didn't see why he couldn't change his original plan and go to Milan after Marrakech instead of before. He explained that he had confirmed a number of meetings that could not be rearranged on such short notice. She was disappointed, but she wasn't angry. The news of her pregnancy had given her power over disappointment. She would cancel their reservation at Riad Madani and delay her trip by a few days. There was no point in going early now. She hoped they could rebook once his work settled down.

The car the El Minzah Hotel had arranged to collect Helen at the Ibn Battouta Airport did not show up, so she hailed a taxi. It had seats upholstered in a worn synthetic leopard cloth that smelled of sweat and stale weed. She rolled the window down to let the air roll over her. There was a message for her at the hotel from William Pauling's secretary. He was indisposed and could not see her in the afternoon as planned but could see her the following morning at eleven.

Accompanied by her notes for the interview and her worn copy of *The Sheltering Sky,* Helen had a late lunch by the pool. She spotted a well-known French philosopher with his wife, who wore a tiny red bikini and moved around the pool as if she were an actress doing multiple takes of the same scene. There was also a gathering of Brits—two young women and two young men slouched on chaises as if they were waiting for something or someone—drinking and talking in loud, sloppy, upper-class accents. All their energy was being spent on making cutting remarks and stretching to be clever. They made her recall the passage she had just read about the difference between a tourist and a traveler—a tourist "accepts his own civilization without question; not so the traveler, who compares it with the others, and rejects those elements he finds not to his liking." Helen judged the people around the pool as tourists, and she did not want to be among them. She returned to her room to lock her passport and wallet in the safe before stopping by the concierge and asking for a map of the city. She wanted to walk around the medina and the English cemetery.

Across from the hotel on Zankat El Houria was the Galerie Delacroix. Next to it was a shop selling beautiful bowls. Their mews house was small and already filled with books and china and furniture she had bought on solitary Saturday afternoons. Buying something for a house they did not own felt like bad luck. When she returned to London, she would make more of an effort to look for a larger place. She would not wait for Christopher.

She spent the rest of the afternoon walking through the medina. It was as if the buildings and houses had been pushed tightly together on narrow streets that rippled down to the sea. The map from the hotel was of no use. The streets hooked and zagged in all directions, disregarding rules of geometry, and the twists and turns and tunnels of the narrow passageways could disorient even the best traveler's sense of direction. Being lost felt joyless without Christopher, and she wasn't quite sure why. She had traveled often by herself. Maybe it was because he had thought that not coming wasn't a big deal. It was as if he had not considered the consequences. She paused to watch a woman getting her hand tattooed with henna. The design was lacelike and extended across her fingers. An assistant shoved a book of designs toward her. Helen shook her head and moved on. As she meandered through the medina she began to feel hot even though the October afternoon was cooling as it leaned toward dusk. The strong scents of cooking—onions and spices and baked bread—pressed down on her and made her feel nauseated. She rested against a building to steady herself. The low sun covered the narrow passageways in shade. She stopped to ask a man who squatted behind embroidered slippers laid in rows on a blanket for the direction to the Grand Socco, but he did not understand and instead picked up the slippers to show her. She kept going.

Around a corner she saw a tight staircase. Maybe it would lead her out of the medina, but it only took her to the top of a building. She could see where she wanted to go. She should be able to find her way out. She climbed down, and when she passed a small shop selling prayer rugs, she stopped and asked again. The man walked with her outside the shop and pointed the way, which was almost at a 120-degree angle to where she thought she should be heading. She walked another several hundred yards along a path that was never straight for very long. She thought she was getting close until she saw the shop where the woman had been getting her hand hennaed. The woman was now paying, the entire top of her hand was covered in an intricate design. Helen asked her if she knew the way out. The woman nodded and indicated she would show her. After a series of twists and turns, the woman stopped and pointed to an opening down a passageway.

On her way back to the hotel, Helen had planned to stop by the English cemetery, but she was followed by several little boys who held their hands out begging for money. They were malnourished, with dark circles under their eyes, their clothes nothing more than dirty rags. She had left her wallet in the safe in her room and had nothing to give them. The small boys tapped the side of her leg in a last desperate plea. She thought of Henry, who was about their age and who was always so well looked after. She would have a child soon. She would go back to the hotel and get some money to give them. After some dead ends and wrong turns, she found her way back to the hotel, but the manager told her that after five in the evening, a woman should not be on the streets unescorted. It was not safe.

There was a message from Christopher. He had called from the Hong Kong airport before he took off for Milan. He would call when he landed.

CHAPTER TWENTY-ONE

DJEMAA EL MOKRA

William Pauling's house was in the hillside suburb of Djemaa el Mokra just west of Tangier. The hotel organized a driver to stay with Helen for the morning. She was at the gate at the appointed time and rang the bell. A voice answered through an intercom and gave instructions to follow once the gate buzzed open. She entered a wild, lush small courtyard with a fishpond in the middle. She did as she was told and arrived at a second gate. Again a bell and intercom, more instructions, this time through an overgrown area of lilac-blue plumbago and citrus trees. The third set of instructions brought her to a front door where a large man stood in the open doorway. "You follow directions well," he said and turned and moved back into the house—expecting her to follow. His action had the same mixture of deliberate weariness and ponderous arrogance as his one-word message scrawled across her letter. It was as if he had recalibrated his life by moving the weight of a metronome to the tip of the pendulum, making all measurement and movement heavy and slow.

She followed him down a dark hallway to a study painted a deep green.

William Pauling had grown up surrounded by beautiful works of art. As a young man, he had wished to acquire pieces of his own, but not being first born, he had received no inheritance, so he became a fine arts dealer with a shop at the seedy end of Pimlico Road. Unable to surround himself with the types of magnificent objects he had grown up with, he had to make choices. Castiglione had always fascinated him, and so he chose to collect only Castiglione at a time when no one cared about his drawings.

"This is the prize of my Castiglione collection," he said, patting the enlarged head of a sheep mounted on a gilt base. The bronze object was a deep, burnished brown, the surface lightly roughed with short marks to replicate the flat hair on a sheep's face. The eyes, by contrast, were smooth, and the reflection caused them to appear lighter than the rest of the head. "It was executed from a design by Castiglione. This is what all the controversy is about. He is about to leave me forever. I am pleased you have seen him."

"I hadn't realized it would be so large," Helen said.

"Oh, yes, all the heads were mounted on human bodies carved out of stone. But we are not to speak about it. It's no matter, for you see, what pleases me most is my collection of drawings of the European Pavilions," he said, pointing to the far wall. "They are what make my heart sing." As he spoke, he moved the palm of his hand upward as if batting a descending balloon. "I collected them first. There were two hundred sets made, and now there are only six known complete ones. Mine is the only one in private hands—the others are held by public museums in New York, Berlin, Dublin, Paris, and Los Angeles. The V&A's set is missing one print. It has been a lifetime of work. I have found them across the world from country house sales in the north of England to dealers in Hong Kong. I even found one in a market stall in Tangier."

Pauling went on to explain how this complex of European Pavilions came to be built in China. In 1747 the Qianlong Emperor saw a painting of a European fountain and asked Castiglione to explain it. Another Jesuit missionary, Father Michel Benoist, had some knowledge of hydraulics and built a model of a fountain. This so delighted the Emperor that he became determined to build both a fountain as well as a European-style pavilion as its setting. "Obviously," Pauling said, waving his hand, "he got carried away. As you know the Qing dynasty emperors built the Yuan Ming Yuan—you may know it by the name the Garden of Perfect Brightness—or the Old Summer Palace as it is called now—as a place to reside and conduct government affairs. The Forbidden City was used only for formal ceremonies. The Qianlong Emperor chose a patch of land in Yuan Ming Yuan to build what I like to call his 'European theme park.' Castiglione was largely responsible for the architecture. Voltaire spoke of it. Victor Hugo equated it to the Parthenon. In fact, he said, and I quote, 'All the treasures of our cathedrals put together could not equal this formidable and splendid museum of the Orient.'" Pauling laughed, pausing with delight. "Imagine." He went around each of the drawings, announcing the names. "Pavilion Harmonizing Surprise and Delight, Observatory of Lands Beyond, Hall of Calm Seas, Observatory of Distant Seas. And here, the most spectacular of the twenty, The Palace of Tranquil Seas. Come closer."

Helen did as she was told. She did not risk telling him she knew everything he was telling her. She had done her research, but she did not want to break the spell.

"The most spectacular of the waterworks was this magnificent clepsydra in front of this pavilion. In the center you see the huge marble shell, and the twelve seated calendrical animals, six on one side, six on the other. The Chinese day was divided into twelve two-hour periods, each represented by one of the twelve animals. The clepsydra was designed so that each head spouted water for its appropriate two-hour period and all twelve heads spouted water at noon." Pauling looked down at her. "It's all quite wonderful, isn't it? You see, here they are." He pointed to the fountain and named the figures in the order they appeared from left to right: dog, rooster, sheep, snake, rabbit, ox, rat, tiger, dragon, horse, monkey, boar.

"I found my sheep thirty-seven years ago. I had just found this print with all the fountains. When I saw the head at a small country house auction not far from where I had been brought up in Wiltshire, I knew I had seen it before. I couldn't place it, but I knew I had to have it. The auctioneers did not know what they had, nor did any of the London dealers who viewed the sale. The auction house thought it was some ill-attempted Victorian copy of something. I bought it for a song. And some time later, as I was admiring my drawing, I made the connection.

"So you see, these pieces call out to one sometimes. When I was younger and much more ambitious, I dreamed of finding all twelve heads and then bequeathing them to the British Museum and having a small room—in my honor, of course"—he laughed in pleasure at the thought—"dedicated to them, with enlarged copies of these drawings as backgrounds. It would have been marvelous, just marvelous," he said, twisting the signet ring on his pinky finger. "But it was not meant to be."

Helen thought Pauling's life seemed to be arranged around the slowed-down curve of beauty. He stopped short of finishing the story, but she knew the rest. The Chinese government had objected to the sale of what they considered looted national property, and the auction house backed down immediately. Eventually Pauling agreed to sell the head to a benefactor of the Chinese government for a fraction of what he would have received had he sold it at auction. She was amazed he still had it. She was surprised he held no bitterness.

"Come," he said, "let us have some sustenance." She followed him to a terrace shaded by large trees where a tray of mint tea had been left. "It reminds me of home," he said when she looked up at the large mulberry tree. "We had the most marvelous mulberry tree in our garden, and in the summers Nanny would send us out to pick bowls and bowls and we would come roaring into the nursery with our bounty, and she would pour cream to the rim and a heaping tablespoon of sugar on top." He pointed to a mosaic on the wall. "First century A.D."

As he was serving tea, Helen asked him if he knew Castiglione's sources for the pavilions.

"Oh, well, he relied on European books available at court and from the missionaries' library. He found inspiration in illustrations of Italian baroque villas, the royal palace and grounds at Versailles, and classical architecture." He answered her question with a boredom it did not deserve. "But I think his design had more to do with homesickness and imagination than about reproducing actual European buildings.

"About homesickness I understand. What I find so remarkable about these prints is that they are one of the first examples of a hybrid Sino-European style. Yi Lantai, who was a member of the China Imperial Academy and who studied under Castiglione, made these drawings. They combine elements of convergent and parallel perspective. Why just look at this one with the enchanting maze. It's the front garden. The major elements of the composition use convergent perspective, the rectangular walled garden enclosing the maze is drawn as a trapezoid, with the back wall shorter than the front. But look—all the paths and partitions of the maze are the same size, they don't get smaller the farther away they are from the front of the maze. All the secondary elements remain the same size, no matter where they are in the drawing.

"You see, the trick in life is learning how to see differently," he said. "Castiglione taught the Chinese about perspective—parallel lines versus converging lines. That's really the trick to life—being able to see both ways and knowing when to switch. In linear, or convergent, perspective, lines that are parallel converge to a single point. In parallel perspective, parallel lines remain the same distance apart whatever their distance from the picture plane. Parallel perspective does not presume a fixed viewpoint as linear perspective does, and objects do not diminish in size because of their distance from the observer. You can be anywhere and the view is the same, but not so with convergent perspective. It assumes a fixed point of observation and that perception will change whenever position changes."

As Pauling was expanding on perspective and explaining how all the drawings had elements of the Western perspective of converging lines, especially in the drawings of the buildings, as well as elements of Chinese perspective, most notably in the way many of the attached gardens included flat planes with no vanishing point or sense of depth, Helen began to feel light-headed and had a metallic taste in her mouth. She tried to stay with him on his ramble. She wondered about the mint tea. She wanted to ask him for a glass of water. She had a hard time concentrating. He had not given her permission to record the interview, so she would not be able to go back over it and pull it apart. After an hour, she wasn't certain she had grasped Pauling's theories, but she had more than enough to write a short article.

From Pauling's house, Helen stopped by the hotel to collect her suitcase and then went directly to the airport. She was happy to be leaving. On the drive to the airport, she thought about the distinctions Pauling had made. Parallel or converging lines. Maybe that was the complexity. If you lived your life along parallel lines, it didn't matter where you stood, things would always look the same. If, on the other hand, you lived your life along converging lines, it did matter where you stood because place determined perspective—standing in one place, things looked one way, in another, a different way. So the trick was to figure out where to stand.

But was that really the right distinction to make? Was she naive to think that marriages and relationships weren't always moving—

either closer together or further apart? Were she and Christopher living along parallel lines? If they were, then it didn't matter where they stood, because no matter where they were, things wouldn't change. That wasn't the way it had been in the beginning. Maybe they had been so in love that they did not even know where they were. Or at least that was the way she had felt about him. But day by day, his work had consumed him—he traveled all week and on most weekends was at the office catching up on the past week, preparing for the next. When they returned from Saint-Tropez, Christopher's business obligations had increasingly begun to edge over into drinks parties and evening events. He understood her work was important, too, and he never pressured her to come with him. But wouldn't it all need to change with a child?

Recently, Christopher had rarely come home before one A.M. He rarely brought up the subject of their having children. When he did, it was at a vague distance, some faraway place in the future. That had to have some significance. Was it indifference or exhaustion? All those late nights—could he be seeing someone? She remembered the lunch at Fiona's where Solange had acted as if a husband's infidelity was a question of when and not if. But Helen wasn't concerned about an affair. It was his indifference, which, for her, felt worse.

CHAPTER TWENTY-TWO

MILAN

Within minutes of arriving at the office, Christopher understood that he should have come earlier. At the close of last year, they had a small operation with one trader and one secretary. Now it appeared the staff had tripled, and he had never been consulted. Before arriving he had reviewed the accounts from the trading business, and staff salaries had not gone up. What was going on? Marc explained that several of the traders were independent and had rented space in their office. Christopher still felt he should have been consulted. As with all analysis, the questions and answers were in the details. "Then why isn't there a line for rental income?" Marc had structured the rent on a quarterly basis. Christopher would see the line item on the next set of accounts. It seemed that Marc had answers for everything.

Christopher and Marc spent the morning reviewing the trading and investment accounts line by line for the year to date. When they went over the list of clients, Christopher noticed that Marc had added several pension funds of large Italian multinationals.

He questioned Marc about what sort of business they were doing for them. Mark said they all had come at the recommendation of Philippe Pavesi.

"How can he generate new business for us? He works for Credit Suisse."

"He left a few months ago and went off on his own. He mainly invests money for a few wealthy individuals. For transactions he can't handle, he brings them to small firms like ours and receives a fee if the deal is successful."

Christopher asked Marc to take him step-by-step through the transactions involving pension funds. Marc explained that, as in the role he had performed for Anthony Wu, he was acting as agent, representing funds in the purchase of parent company shares. The only difference was that he was now on the buy side and not on the sell side. Under U.K. law, a company could not give financial assistance for the purchase of its own shares, and Christopher assumed that similar restrictions applied across the E.U. They would need to determine that there was no collusion between trustees of the pension funds and the company. Also by U.K. law, the trustees had to be independent and have no association with the company. Christopher was concerned that some of the more aggressive Italian CEOs could use this strategy to prop up their share prices by having their pension funds buy shares from time to time. It could be used as a form of stock manipulation.

He was beginning to question whether they should have such a close association with Philippe. He had agreed with Marc that Mr. Pavesi's rumored transgressions had nothing to do with his son. But now he was not so sure. It was beginning to feel like spilled water. It could only be a matter of time before it seeped across a line.

Christopher told Marc he was going to bring in outside counsel to review the trades just to make certain. Their firm had been going so well, there was no need to take on extra risk for higher gains, especially if the activities brought them too close to any line that, if crossed, could jeopardize their firm's reputation. He would ask their U.K. counsel, Nigel Barrington, to oversee everything. Christopher could tell that Marc was angered by his unilateral action and was trying not to show it because he knew he had no choice but to consent.

Marc invited him to his flat for a drink before dinner. Christopher arrived early, and a butler answered the door. The flat was much grander than he was expecting. He and Marc had done well but not well enough to support this style of living, and he knew Ghislaine had no money. In fact, Marc had told him so when he had recommended paying Ghislaine a design fee for the interior decoration of their new office. Christopher was shown to the drawing room and offered a drink before Marc came down. The room was stylish, with a combination of antique and modern furniture and works of art. A Jim Dine dressing gown hung over an Italian painted eighteenth-century console table. A mounted scagliola panel was surrounded by modern art deco sofas. Ghislaine knew what she was doing. He wandered around looking at all the photographs—mainly of their wedding in Rome, on a boat somewhere, on the terrace at Il Pellicano. One of the wedding photos surprised him. There next to Marc at the altar was Philippe Pavesi.

While he was waiting for Marc, he checked his phone. Nothing from Helen. He left her another message and then called the hotel in Tangier. He was surprised to learn she had checked out. He reached her at home. She said she had decided to come back a day early—she had gotten what she needed—she wasn't feeling great and was happy to be home.

Marc appeared. Ghislaine would not be joining them. She was still nursing their baby and was exhausted. He had invited Philippe instead. They had a quick drink and walked down the street to Savini next to the Duomo. The evening air was chilly with a light drizzle. On the way to the restaurant Marc complained about the autumn weather as a way of filling the silence between them.

During dinner, Philippe explained a tax straddle that had been very successful in the U.S. in avoiding income taxes. It had recently been shut down. Philippe thought it could be applied with modification to the European markets. The controversy in the United States had centered around whether or not certain transactions had economic risk. Christopher listened carefully but was very clear he opposed even considering pursuing Philippe's idea, which was based, as far as he could surmise, on breaking the spirit of the law while staying within the letter of it.

After a full review of the trading records with U.K. and Italian counsel and accountants, Christopher came across nothing illegal. There were certain actions and trades that pushed the boundaries—there was no question the practices were very aggressive—but they all held up in the light of day. Senior accountants from the top firm in Milan had gone through past and proposed transactions step-by-step. Sloppy accounting was the most they could find. Not only did the head of the securities department say the transactions were within the law, but also he said his firm would provide an opinion letter to this effect. Every objection Christopher had put up, Marc had been able to extinguish, but despite legal reassurances, Christopher remained uneasy. Maybe it all had to do with the difference between the disposition of an investor and the disposition of a trader.

CHAPTER TWENTY-THREE

LONDON

The following day, Helen made an appointment to see her doctor. The metallic taste would not go away. The ultrasound showed the sac but no heartbeat. She asked him to check again, maybe the ultrasound had not picked it up, but he shook his head and told her what was going to happen. She should undergo a procedure to avoid having to go through the experience of passing the fetus. Each day was adding more risk that she could abort anytime.

"And there couldn't be another one?"

"No, dear. Twins are always a possibility but there was only one fetus." He moved the handle of the ultrasound monitor around her stomach to show her the outline of the uterus. "There is nothing more here. If it would put your mind at rest, come back tomorrow, but it won't change the results."

Helen tried to push past her doctor's logic, but it caught her no matter where she turned. Still, the following morning she arrived at his office. Again, there was no heartbeat. She felt as if her body no longer belonged to her.

"You've waited long enough. You could abort anytime now. We should schedule a D&C as soon as possible." When she didn't say anything, he added, "Without one, there's the danger of hemorrhaging and infection if all the tissue is not expelled."

She asked him again about the hep A vaccine. He gave her the same answer as before—it was highly unlikely it had caused the miscarriage.

"Then could it have been something I drank? When I was in Morocco I was served a mint tea that made me feel strange."

"Very, very doubtful. I'm sure it's not because of the vaccine or something you ingested. It's Mother Nature's way."

"You can't tell anything from the embryo?"

"No, dear. This happens more than you know. Most women never know they've had a miscarriage because it happens so early in the pregnancy."

"And you're one hundred percent certain?"

"Yes. You should have no issues about getting pregnant again if that is what you wish."

At six A.M. Helen drove herself to the clinic and checked in. Her doctor came by to see her and told her she would be out around ten A.M. He asked if her husband had come, and she said no, he was out of the country on business. She lied and said she had a friend coming to pick her up.

She woke up in the recovery room feeling as if she were underwater. Everything took effort. She tried to keep her eyes open, but her eyelids felt waterlogged. She tried to sit up, but she felt as if the air were so heavy it was pinning her down. She didn't have the strength to push past it. She rested a bit more, then tried again. She was desperate to go home. The discharging nurse was insistent someone had to drive her home. Helen hadn't made any arrangements, her friends would be at work. She asked if they could call a cab. The nurse called, they were in the middle of morning rush hour, there was a forty-minute wait. Helen couldn't bear to stay in the hospital waiting room—it smelled of warmed-over chicken broth and antiseptic. She didn't want to call a girlfriend—there would be too many questions. She would call Peregrine. She wasn't even sure he still had a car, but he would be too awkward to ask her any questions. He answered after two rings. No, he didn't have a car but he could borrow his flatmate's and be there "in a jif."

Peregrine pulled up in a vintage Mini Cooper. "Your ladyship," he said, running around to open the car door for her. He was wearing the pea-green coat he had admired in the Saint-Tropez market.

"Peregrine, you bought the coat."

"I wore it just for you. Thought you might need some cheering up. Your ladyship is looking very pale. Could I give you my coat?"

Helen shook her head and clipped her seat belt.

"Are you up for a coffee or a spot of lunch?"

"If you could just take me home."

"I take it there's nothing seriously wrong?"

"No, nothing seriously wrong, but I'd rather not talk about it."

"By the way," he said, as they were turning the corner to her house, "Zara's invited us all to a reading at the Royal Society of Literature tomorrow evening. Want to come?"

"Thanks, Peregrine, maybe a rain check. I think I should take it easy for a few days. I think Christopher may be coming back. By the way," she said as she got out of the car, "I'm glad you got the coat."

He laughed. "I knew you'd come around."

Helen changed into her pajamas. She planned to stay in bed all day and watch television. Despite what her doctor had said about her ability to get pregnant again, she felt defeated and inadequate. She didn't call Christopher, even though she wanted to. It was her way of proving to herself that she didn't need him. He never worried about her. He always assumed she would be fine.

Christopher had tried Helen from his hotel before he left for the airport. When she didn't answer, he assumed she was in the shower or had gone for a run. He kept trying her cell on his way to the airport and still no answer. His flight was boarding when he arrived, but he hung back to try her one more time. She finally picked up.

"I've been trying to reach you. Where are you?"

She didn't say anything. She allowed herself to misinterpret his concern as a reprimand.

"Are you okay?" His voice slowed and dropped down a register.

"Yeah, fine."

"Helen, talk to me. Are you sick?"

"No, I just don't feel great."

The airport loudspeaker announcing the last call for his flight prevented them from speaking.

"Where are you?"

"At the airport. I'm flying back to London—hang on one second—yes, I'm coming—listen, Helen, I'm going to have to turn my phone off in a minute. I was going to go into the office when I landed, but I'll come home."

"No, don't. I think I'm just going to try to sleep."

"Shouldn't you see a doctor? Helen, are you there?"

"Yeah. No, I don't need to see a doctor." God, were they disconnected. She wasn't going to tell him about the miscarriage now. She was thinking about how they seemed to be moving away from each other and wondering why neither one of them tried to do anything about it. There were times when it felt as if he had lost her, as if he were thinking so intensely about what was in front of him that he would forget her, as if his mind were emptied of all thoughts of her. When she first noticed it, she interpreted it as the "eye-on-the-object look" Auden had written about, but Auden had been describing the rapt expression of a cook, a surgeon, a clerk—the forgetting of themselves as they performed a function. But forgetting oneself was different from forgetting another person. She had been disappointed, but she had not been surprised when Christopher couldn't meet her in Marrakech. She wondered if he had ever planned to come. Had he only been humoring her by pretending he would make it?

"Are you sure you're okay?"

"I'm fine."

"Okay. I'll be home early evening. I love—"

She hung up before he could finish his sentence.

Her abruptness unsettled him. Her disappointments always moved on like patches of weather, but this one felt set in. He knew she had wanted him to meet her in Morocco. Maybe it was the disappointment of not being able to write the larger article. She had been excited by the complexity of the research. A profile of an aesthete was something she could do without thinking. Christopher had told her nothing about what he was going through, partly because he didn't want to worry her and partly because it was easier not to. He was looking forward to being with her next weekend, even if it was at Charlotte and Eric's. He hoped they wouldn't have every moment of the weekend scheduled. On the way in from the airport he would stop to see if he could find something to cheer her up.

"*Timeo Danaos et dona ferentes,*" Christopher said, holding up a book, a bottle of wine, and a white paper bag with the name of her favorite restaurant on it. He found Helen lying in bed watching television.

"I know what that means. You're not Greek."

"I know but I don't know the word for *banker* in Latin."

"Argentarius."

"Timeo argentarios et dona ferentes."

He kissed her. "Completely pathetic kiss," he said and wouldn't let her go. "Three gifts! Stop being mad at me."

"I'm not mad."

"Oh, yes you are. Are you okay?"

She shrugged her shoulders. "I'll feel better tomorrow."

"Which one do you want first? All will bring you pleasure. Missed your chance, I'll choose. Book first," he said, handing her a small package wrapped in tan tissue paper. "You have no idea how much trouble I went to to get this for you."

She carefully unwrapped the book. It was slight—the size of a prayer book, brick colored, with an embossed anthemion design in the center of the cover and a black floral band above and below. *Ins and Outs of Circus Life or Forty-Two Years Travel of John H. Glenroy, Bareback Rider, Through United States, Canada, South America and Cuba.* "Is this Édouard's?"

"No, but he told me where I might find one. I basically had to sell part of my soul to convince the clerk at Heywood Hill to part with it. Apparently requests for books on circuses are not as rare as you might imagine. I'm not the only one in London who thinks he works in a three-ring circus. Have a look." He pointed with his chin to the book she had just put on her bedside table. "And for this," he said, holding up the paper bag, "I bargained with what remained of my soul. The maître d' pretended not to understand my request. I'll be back with dinner. We'll save the wine for when you're better."

She opened the book. Inside she found a handwritten note by the author to the buyer along with a notice of "The Broadway Circus: Novelty Is the Spice of Life," which had been cut out of a newspaper. "Master Glenroy will appear on his rapid courser. The act of this youth must be seen to be believed." She started to read the first page. "I was born 1828, in the City of Washington, D.C., but when just two years old, having lost both my parents, I was removed to Baltimore, and adopted by a lady named Hannah Murdock. . . . After attaining the age of four, I commenced to show a great liking for horses, and also for all kinds of acrobatic exercise, which grew stronger as I continued to grow older." Why did it have to start with a small child? She closed the book and put it down. She wiped her face and turned back to the television.

CHAPTER TWENTY-FOUR

EASTTHORPE

Eastthorpe Hall was, as Fiona had described it, a grand estate built in the late 1700s, which sat in the middle of twelve thousand acres. The drive dipped and turned to give glimpses and teases of the Grade I listed house until, three hundred yards from the house, it straightened out into a beech-lined avenue that ran directly on axis with a walled driving court.

"I think I should tell Eric that the driveway is not long enough," Christopher said. "I'm guessing we might make housefall by midnight."

Helen laughed. "It is ridiculously long."

"Seriously, what will you give me if I make that suggestion? I should get extra credit if I can do it with a straight face."

"I'm not going to encourage your bad behavior."

Their arrival had been announced. As they pulled up to the house, Eric and Charlotte were followed by a staff of twelve lined up to greet them. *Oh, God,* Helen thought. *They are going to unpack for us*. She regretted how hastily she had thrown everything into their cases. She leaned toward Christopher and whispered, "Someone needs to tell them hardly anyone—maybe even no one—in England does this anymore."

Charlotte showed them to their large room, furnished with a four-poster bed with a sagging mattress, a sofa, a pair of chairs, and a skirted dressing table, all covered in the same floral chintz.

"Are these the original furnishings?" Helen asked.

"Well, at least original to the Bolton family."

Helen walked over to the window and looked closely at the fabric. The small sprigs and butterflies reminded her of a piece of cloth she had seen in the Foundling Hospital binders. She thought she had seen the room before. "Wasn't this house featured . . ."

"On the cover of *The World of Interiors*—May of last year. Of course, we will change everything once Mario develops his plan—but don't tell poor Anthony. He thinks we intend to keep everything as it is."

Charlotte encouraged them to hurry. Everyone was already gathering in the library for drinks. Dinner would be served at nine.

When Charlotte left, Christopher stretched out on the bed, his hands locked beneath his head. "Certainly seen better days. I may end up crippled by morning."

"Shh." Helen laughed, partly amused and partly irritated. "Get up. Charlotte made it clear everyone is waiting for us."

He looked mournfully at her. "Fair to say they've been watching too many episodes of that television series on English country life."

"They really are trying to out-English the English."

"Someone needs to tell them to stop. I wonder if they will get dogs. That will be the real test, but it only counts if the dogs are allowed inside the house."

Helen was surprised and delighted to see Solange and Anthony. She told Solange about her visit with William Pauling. Her piece would be out soon. Charlotte introduced Christopher and Helen to an American couple who now lived in Geneva; a South American businessman, Carlos Muñoz; a Canadian couple who lived in London, whom Helen recognized from society page photographs; Mario, the interior designer, and Jasper, a young man plucked from the Sotheby's training program to serve as Charlotte and Eric's curator.

The assembled group were discussing Venice and Florence. The American, who, as Helen observed over the course of the evening, held only immutable opinions, said that he loved Venice and that his wife loved Florence, and it was his experience with married couples that one was always a lover of Florence, the other a lover of Venice. One loved order and kept everything neat while the other loved romance and disorder. When the Canadian woman said that both she and her husband loved Venice, he pronounced that their offspring would not genetically progress.

Helen noticed that Christopher spent dinner listening to the businessman seated to his left and ignored the custom of turning after each course. As the man who loved Venice bombarded her with strong declarative statements, Helen partially listened to Christopher and Carlos's conversation about business and attractive deals in South America, all involving some form of monopoly. She was reminded of Édouard Beaumont's comment about Christopher being good at listening.

At the end of dinner, Eric led all the men into the library to smoke cigars, and Charlotte rescued the decorator and asked him to give the ladies a tour of the ground floor.

When the tour ended, Charlotte led everyone back to the library. Eric, pleased with his Cuban cigars and even more pleased that everyone was enjoying themselves so much, waved Charlotte good night. The "boys" were going to stay up late and have another glass of port.

Helen was angry Christopher decided not to come to bed with her. Did he ever put them first? She had imagined that they would have time to themselves. She had wanted to tell him how happy she had been to learn she was pregnant, and she wanted his reassurance that he had wanted this, too. She wanted to tell him how she had felt when the heartbeat could not be found. She wanted to tell him everything for the first time. She waited up for him, but the longer she waited, the more resolved she became that she would never bring the subject up. Absolutes were fortifications—she understood that—but still she would not let this go. She tried to shift her mind to other topics, but she was unable to sleep, and when Christopher returned just before two A.M. she was still awake, but she did not acknowledge his presence. She carried her anger with her to the next morning.

"Would you ever want to live like this?" Christopher asked, feeling her coolness as they dressed for breakfast. He knew she would not be able to resist answering.

"Zero interest—possessions possess. Charlotte didn't grow up like this, did she?"

"Not at all. I think money was quite tight, which is probably why she likes all this so much."

"At times she seems almost giddy with it. She was going on and on about how difficult customs officials can be about private—"

"Did you happen to speak at all to Carlos?"

Helen was irritated he had cut her off. "The South American? No, why? Weren't you sitting next to him in the library last night?"

"Carlos said he had met me in Bermeja last Christmas but I don't remember him. Do you?"

"No, but maybe he was at one of the drinks parties we went to."

"He said he had invested with our firm, and he fully expected me to know that. I don't even recognize his name. If he's such a prominent client as he indicated, it's very strange Marc has never mentioned him. I was just with Marc going over all the new accounts, and the name Carlos Muñoz never came up. There's something about him that doesn't add up."

"Did you ask him how he knows Eric?"

"He was vague, said something about investing with him in Mexico or that they'd looked at some investments together." Christopher would speak to Carlos at breakfast and press further.

When they arrived at breakfast, Charlotte informed Christopher that Carlos had flown back to London early in the morning and had asked Charlotte to give Christopher his regards. After breakfast, Eric led everyone on a walk to see the stables and pastures that were the planned site of his soon-to-be-built private golf course. A very English lunch was followed by a tour of the operations behind Eastthorpe's shoot. Eric arrived in a brand-new, unmuddied black supercharged Range Rover and asked Christopher to drive with him. Helen thought he looked like a little boy who had just stolen his parents' car. *Doesn't he know he can raise the seat?* she thought to herself. *Does he even know how to shoot?*

Later, Christopher confirmed that Eric did not know how to shoot. But he was certain that Eric would learn quickly, assuming, of course, he didn't get shot first. "His instinctive will to kill, assuming he has any kind of eye at all, will be harnessed in no time at all." Christopher also told Helen there was a reason Eric had wanted to drive with him. "He told me if we ever wanted to sell our firm, I should come to him first. I thought a weekend just for pleasure was unusual for him."

"What did you tell him?"

"I told him we weren't interested in making any changes now, but if anything were to change, I would let him know."

"You wouldn't . . ."

"No, of course not. I was just being polite. He thinks the entire world is for sale. But the best news of the weekend—Eric said that Bermeja was too primitive for him."

"How could he say that?"

"Doubted they would ever go back. Much better for us that he needs to work on his aim." Christopher had gotten Helen to laugh, and her laughter pushed them forward.

The evening was an American barbecue with a pig and a lamb on a spit. A number of couples invited from neighboring estates came to meet the American who had paid the highest price ever for a shooting estate. Eric had flown over a U.S. line-dancing champion, who stood in the ballroom and offered to give guests slow and simple instructions. Eric "borrowed" Christopher to discuss some matter, Charlotte declared herself too uncoordinated, and the other guests were afraid of embarrassing themselves. Helen felt badly for the instructor, who stood alone, so she gathered up Solange and Anthony and a couple from a neighboring estate and told them it was fun, like a Scottish reel. Soon the instructor had two lines of five following her lead. Solange and Helen took a break and left Anthony on his fourth attempt to follow the simple steps of "Achy Breaky Heart."

"Much more fun than Scottish reeling," Solange declared. She asked Helen how Christopher had liked Marrakech, and Helen said that he had been unable to go—something had come up. "My dear, when do the two of you ever spend time together?" She did not know how to take Solange's words—were they an innocent observation or an indirect warning?

CHAPTER TWENTY-FIVE

LONDON

Solange's question still echoed in Helen's mind months later as she walked down the King's Road. She tried to answer the question in ways that satisfied her, but they all fell short. Too often, when they went out in the evening, the dinners were business related and she would find herself seated next to a chief executive or finance director with whom she had nothing in common. The American businessmen were the worst. They described their multiple homes—apartments on Fifth or Park Avenue in New York City, beach houses in the Hamptons, seaside villas in St. Barts, ranches in Wyoming—she doubted if they even knew their way around a horse. It was as if they were playing some grown-up version of King of the Castle. They spoke about their art collections as if pieces of sports equipment. Worse still were their discussions of their private planes. Helen learned early that as long as the conversation remained solely focused on them, they would tell Christopher after dinner what a charming wife he had. The conversations were all variations of the one she'd had one evening at an exhibit of contemporary artists at the Tate. She had sat between the treasurer of a U.K. publishing company and the chief executive of a well-known hedge fund.

"I have a great way of explaining numbers to children," the chief executive said. "For example, I tell them the way to think about one million and one billion. One million represents twelve days, and one billion represents thirty-three years." His wife was keen for him to write a children's book so that other children could benefit from his explanations. He asked Helen if she knew any good writers. He said he knew there would be plenty who would appreciate the "extra dough."

Thinking about writers, Helen remembered some reviews of novels that had sounded interesting and thought she would pick out a few for the summer holiday. It was a late April day, and the King's Road was crowded with people shopping and running errands. She cut down an alleyway to John Sandoe Books to escape the crammed sidewalks. She liked the slow-tapping-castanets sound of her boot heels on the pavement. Édouard Beaumont had offered them La Mandala for a second summer, and Christopher had taken it without asking her. And even though she resented his not asking her, she was looking forward to going. She made her selection and then found a small café to have a coffee and examine her purchases. The friends Helen could meet for lunch or a coffee on Saturday were evaporating, as many of them now had small children, and Saturdays were exhausted with errands and children's activities.

Someone dropped a backpack in the seat across from her. She looked up. It was Nick van Asten.

"Long time no see."

"Nick." She stood up and kissed him hello.

Helen and Nick had briefly overlapped at the paper. Within a year after she started, he went off on his own as a freelance photographer. His decision had worked out well for him, and he was now represented by a Chelsea gallery. He said he had just gotten back from two weeks in Calais and before that three weeks in Tanzania. He said he was looking forward to being around London for a while. He asked Helen what she had been up to. He had heard she had gotten married. She told him she had seen his image of the man trying to catch a ride on the back of a truck. "Refugee camps are becoming my specialty," he laughed. "Everyone is pretending it's not a problem, but there's a shanty town developing. It's rough and these immigrants are desperate. When the trucks are in slow lines, they crawl under the trucks and hold on to the underbelly and stay there if they can until the truck crosses into England. Do you know how dangerous that is?" She remembered now that Nick always seemed to speak as if he were running down a hill.

"Hey, want another coffee?" Nick asked, standing up.

"Why don't we work on something together?" he said as he sat back down. "You could write an article for the *Times* on the situation in Calais. It's getting worse, not better. I'll go with you and show you around. That is, as long as you agree to use my images." He smiled to acknowledge he already had his answer. "People need to start thinking about these people. They have a desperateness that you and I will never know." He said he was making another trip in August. Why didn't she come with him? She said she would bring it up with her editor, but even if he liked the idea, the only time Christopher could take off was August, when all his clients were on holiday. And it wasn't as if she would be in Calais for the entire month. "Just for a few days," he said as they were leaving the coffee shop. She could do the research before and after the trip.

"Come over and I'll show you what I have. Here," he said, turning her wrist over and writing his number. "Don't worry"—he spoke with the cap of his pen between his teeth. "Everything about me washes off."

When she was halfway down the block he called to her, "Helen, don't forget to call me."

God, was he a flirt, she thought as she walked home. She looked at the numbers he had written on the inside of her wrist. Running into Nick had felt strangely luxurious, and she had done nothing to discourage him.

CHAPTER TWENTY-SIX

SAINT-TROPEZ

David was blunt with Helen. He was not going to send her—no matter who the photographer was. "It's like sending you to a war zone, and you're not a journalist who covers conflicts. You have no idea how dangerous it can get—it can turn in a minute. Some of the refugees have been brutally murdered, and a student journalist was savagely raped two months ago. Besides, I hear the *Guardian* may have a large piece coming out. Find something else to do with Nick. On second thought, don't—it's double danger—he sleeps with every female journalist he works with."

"Oh, come on, David."

"It's not you I'm worried about. I've been thinking about assigning a piece on Cuba. Any interest? You could take Christopher. I'd feel better if you were with someone."

"Sure, just let me know." She wasn't getting her hopes up, about either the article or Christopher, but as she walked out of David's office she remembered the small book Christopher had given her on the circus performer. On the last pages was an account of the cities, listed by year, where he had spent each New Year's Day, Fourth of July, and Christmas over a forty-year span. He had spent considerable time in Cuba.

Christopher canceled all but one and a half weeks of their holiday in Saint-Tropez. He had to go to Hong Kong for a board meeting. He explained to Helen that the Chinese, unlike the rest of Europe, did not take August off. He also had planned a trip to New York City to meet with Dan O'Connor, a former classmate from Oxford, a Rhodes scholar who had recently left his job as an assistant U.S. attorney and was about to join a top New York City law firm as a litigator. Christopher remained concerned about Marc's trading activities. He couldn't point to anything specific, it was just a feeling he had. And Carlos Muñoz's comments had intensified his suspicions. He wanted to discuss his concerns with Dan before he started with his new law firm to avoid any possible conflicts of interest.

Christopher insisted there was no reason for Helen to cut her holiday short. She should stay at La Mandala and invite friends or family. He was certain her brothers and their wives would enjoy coming down. Since her miscarriage, being around her nieces and nephews made her wonder if she would ever have children, and she did not like the feelings that crept in around that question. But she could not tell him this. As time had passed, the significance of her not telling him had expanded. Distance had taken on a weight of its own and she did not want to acknowledge it. And yet the idea of being at La Mandala without him made her feel desolate. She would come with him to New York, she could find things to do during the day. Willie's new play was now in rehearsal, and she wanted to see it. Christopher warned her that New York in August was the last place most people wanted to be.

The second summer in Saint-Tropez was more fun than she had

imagined—partly because there were no houseguests and partly because Édouard left them his Riva. For those eleven days, they only traveled by foot or boat. In the mornings they took day trips, west to explore the islands of Porquerolles, Port-Cros, and the Île du Levant and east to the Lérins Islands.

"I'm surprised more people aren't here," Helen said when they had anchored on the south side of Île Sainte-Marguerite and walked across the narrow island to Fort Royal.

"Looks as if there will be soon." Christopher pointed east to a large boat chugging toward them from Cannes. They walked around the star-shaped fort where they had come to see the cell of the Man in the Iron Mask. They found it down a corridor of six cells. Heavy, dark, iron-studded doors opened onto a room larger than they had expected. On the north wall, a window was covered by three iron grills with small square openings. A fireplace was on one side of the window, a latrine on the other. The floor was covered in small square terra-cotta tiles. The cell was strangely comforting. Christopher walked to the window and watched the tour boat dock. Helen ran her hands along the wall, feeling for secrets.

"Ready to go?" he asked. They both wanted to leave before the passengers arrived. They walked to a patisserie and bought sandwiches and bottles of water. He looked at a map. "Same way back or different?"

"Different."

They walked west around the perimeter of the island and found a natural beach, to sit and eat their sandwiches. She read the brochure they had been given with the tickets to the fort. "They still don't know who he was."

"The Man in the Iron Mask?"

"Yes, but this says it was black velvet."

"I'm feeling a little better about him already," Christopher said. "I mean, peace and quiet, room with a view of the Côte d'Azur, fireplace, velvet versus iron—"

"Stop. Aren't you the least bit curious about him?"

"Not anymore. Every French schoolboy at some point has to write about Jules Verne or Jacques Cousteau or the Man in the Iron Mask. You know, if your theory about emotions left in one place is correct, you could test it out here. If they really do stay where they are experienced, then you might be able to detect their presence and match them up with one of the suspects. Judging from this," he said, taking the pamphlet from her, "there are, at this point in time, at least"—he paused to count—"seven possible candidates."

"First of all," she said, taking the pamphlet back, "it has to be your own emotions. I never said you could discover someone else's. And secondly, even if I could tell who it was, I would then become so wildly sought after that I'm not sure I would have time for you."

"That would be tragic."

"Would it?"

"Helen, why are you saying that?"

"It's been hard finding time with you. I mean this holiday has been great, but I know when it's over and we go back . . ."

"Look, I know it's been tough, and I know the goalposts keep changing, and now I've got to get to the bottom of my concerns about Marc. But if you want me to walk away, I'll do it. I really mean that. But if I stay in, then it's going to be bad for a bit longer. And I know we've talked about having kids—it's just right now we don't see each other enough, and adding kids would only make it worse."

"What does 'a while' mean?"

"Hard to say—six months, a year, but I'm guessing."

"If you did walk away, what would you do?"

"I don't know, I haven't thought about it. I could always go back to law of some kind, maybe a smaller firm."

"I wouldn't do that—ask you to leave your firm. I know how hard you've worked, and I know how much you love it, I see it. I wouldn't ask you to do that for me. I'm not asking you to do something that drastic, but I wish we could be together more. I don't think I'm asking that much."

"I understand and I will try, I promise."

"David asked me if I wanted to write a piece on Cuba. I have an idea about going to the places I read about in that book you gave me on the circus performer."

"I meant it as a metaphor."

"I know, but it's a moving story. Maybe you'll come with me. I'd like to travel around the country. You could help me. Very few people speak English."

"I might be able to in January or February—it just depends on what's going on."

In the evening, they walked into town and had dinner at the Moroccan restaurant they had gone to with Édouard. Helen had wanted to go to a different one, but it was the middle of August and everything had been booked for weeks. Édouard always had a table at La Salama because he was a friend of the owner, and Danny was able to get them in. They were given a table outside in the courtyard underneath an old olive tree. A stone bench ran the length of the courtyard walls, with tables for two to eight arranged along the inside perimeter. The seats and tables were low, and Christopher sat next to her so he could stretch out his legs. Last summer's brightly colored cushions and pillows had been replaced with ones that were all white. The simplicity of the stone and white fabric reminded Helen of the cottage where they had stayed in Majorca. She forgot about Morocco. Christopher ordered a bottle of wine he recognized as being from the vineyard of the monastery on Île Saint-Honorat, the island next to Île Sainte-Marguerite. They started with grilled peppers and shared a tagine of chicken with olive and lemon.

During dinner, she told him more about John Glenroy. "When he was seven he was playing on the streets of Baltimore doing small acrobatic tricks to amuse his friends, and a man saw him and asked him if he wanted to join the circus. When Glenroy said yes, the man went to his foster mother and asked for permission. Glenroy writes that he was delighted because he thought circus life would be 'a life of pleasure where everyday was sunshine and with never a cloud.' But it wasn't. He learned to do a backward flip on a cantering horse by first practicing on a barn beam. If he fell, he would get whipped. And he writes about this in a voice that is flat and uninflected. Doesn't that strike you as strange?"

"I suppose in some ways emotions are luxuries—doesn't sound as if he could allow himself any."

"And despite being with circuses most of his life, they were always disbanding and forming new groups so he was never with the same people for very long. At the back of the volume he included a list of the twenty-four managers he had served under. And I've been thinking, why? To document their existence—unlikely any of them would have been alive when his book was published. A message in a bottle to any other performers he had traveled with? What purpose did it serve? He mentioned no friends or acquaintances—only one family, the Cardenas family in Cuba. When he was ten, a man from a rival circus tried to kidnap him, and he ran to their house and asked for safety. The Marquis de Cardenas was particularly kind to him and offered him shelter."

"Are you going to try to find any descendants of that family?"

"I'll try. I would think there would be a record of them somewhere. I'm not sure how important they were to him, but they were important enough for him to mention. But having no parents or extended family, never marrying, never having a home, always being on the road, the past was, in a way, all he had to define who he was. It was as if the past were Glenroy's only true companion. And yet, while his memory was so exact about the names of people and the identities of places, it was a memory so impersonal, so outside of himself, that it could have belonged almost to anyone, or at least parts of it. At the back of the slim volume was a list of the places where Glenroy and his troupe performed on New Year's Day, July Fourth, and Christmas for over forty years. Why did he choose to document those holidays—days most people spend with family?" Helen asked not expecting to receive an answer. "Did Glenroy's lists assume that memory of dates and places could stand in for affection, as surrogates for family, or do you think he reduced his experience to a set of numbers and dates as a way of making it accessible to others?"

"Maybe lists gave him immunity from loneliness. Maybe that's all there was to it," Christopher said. He hadn't read Glenroy's account, but he seemed to have a more intuitive understanding of him than she did.

A few days before they left, Helen walked down to the market to buy lavender soap to bring back to her mother. The vendors in the market were packing up for the day, but she managed to find what she wanted. She took the long way home through the small streets and alleyways as a way of saying good-bye to the town. As she passed by some of the shops she had taken Ghislaine to the previous summer, it was as if she had conjured her spirit. From a distance, she saw Ghislaine with another woman leaving a boutique with large shopping bags. They were heading to the port.

"You'll never believe who I saw," Helen said to Christopher, whom she found reading by the pool. "Ghislaine. She was walking out of one of the shops I took her to last summer. She was with another woman who looked like the new wife of Edward Farringdon." Helen referred to the man who was the controlling shareholder of the paper where she worked.

"Probably was. Marc said they were spending a week with them on their boat."

Helen was astounded. How had Ghislaine and Marc become such good friends with the Farringdons? As far as she knew, they didn't run in the same circles.

"Did you say hello?"

"No, they were a block away and heading in the opposite direction—down to the port. Is Edward Farringdon a client?"

"No, but we wish he were. He deals almost exclusively with Goldman."

"Marc and Ghislaine being invited for a week—doesn't that surprise you?"

"Not really. The friendship could have come through Ghislaine and Farringdon's wife. Maybe they knew each other before—they're probably about the same age, and Ghislaine is very focused on being in the right circles. Plus, she knows she will please Marc by being friends with women married to powerful and rich men. Marc said Farringdon's boat is amazing. It's a classic sailing boat designed by one of the top shipbuilding firms in Italy. Apparently it's made from the most beautiful wood."

"But don't you think it's strange that Marc is here and he hasn't let you know?"

"I didn't make any effort to invite them here or suggest we get together."

What Christopher didn't tell Helen was that Marc had asked Édouard about renting La Mandala for the month of August. He had learned about Marc's inquiry from Édouard. At the time, Christopher didn't tell Helen because he knew she wouldn't let it go. He didn't want to spend his energy on the topic. To give Marc the benefit of the doubt, Christopher had been so vague about his summer plans that Marc could have understood they wouldn't be taking La Mandala. But whatever the understanding, Marc still should have come to him first.

The day before they were supposed to fly to New York, Danny found Christopher and Helen by the pool. A storm was gathering power as it moved across southern France. It was a bad one, Danny said. The winds were predicted to exceed eighty kilometers per hour. Flights from Nice were expected to be canceled. They were not saying how long it would last, could be a day, but he had seen them last as long as a week.

Christopher was irritated. He didn't want to cancel his dinner with Dan O'Connor. He went inside to check on their flight. He returned and told Helen they should be fine. The mistral wasn't expected to arrive for another day or two. He sat back in his chair and picked up the newspaper. "We should have no problem leaving tomorrow. Our flight is fine."

She asked him what a mistral was, and he explained that in the Mediterranean there were at least eight different types of winds. He knew the names of the winds as if they were points on a compass. He traced an imaginary eight-point compass on her back. "From the north, Tramontane, beyond the mountain; northeast, Gregale, the wind that wrecked the apostle Paul's ship; Levanter, from the east; southeast, Sirocco, which brings with it the sands from North Africa; south, Ostro; southwest, Libeccio; west, Ponente; and last but not least, from the northwest, the Mistral, which we will happily miss."

"How do you know all this?" she asked.

"The sea captain who looked after the land in Bermeja had it tattooed in the middle of his back. I spent hours walking behind him."

CHAPTER TWENTY-SEVEN

NEW YORK

Helen had spent the first two days walking around New York City, going to museums and dropping by galleries manned by young interns who believed that anyone remaining in New York in August was, by definition, disqualified from buying art. At the gift shops of MoMA and the Met, she looked for a present for her eldest brother Louis's forty-fifth birthday but she found nothing that would interest him. He collected wine and first editions of Trollope. When she returned to London she would check with Max and Theo to see what they had chosen. Maybe they could give him something together.

She made it to the roof garden of the Metropolitan Museum where the British sculptor Andy Goldsworthy had constructed two eighteen-foot domes of wood in the shape of large igloos. Inside the structures were tall columns of balanced stones. The domes were made from split rails assembled so that the stone columns could be glimpsed from the spaces between the rails. She thought about the *palapas* in Bermeja and the afternoon Christopher had fallen asleep under a pergola where the sun had shadowed stripes across his back. She longed to be surrounded by those lush pinks and greens and blues. Goldsworthy's desiccated domes and stone columns felt disconnected from any sense of life, and she did not stay on the roof garden long.

"Three days of rain," Helen said to Christopher as she looked out the hotel window down to the street. Tops of umbrellas hugged the sides of buildings and bunched on street corners.

He looked up from gathering papers for his upcoming meeting. "It looks set in." He asked her about the details of Willie's play they were planning to attend.

"It's being held in the basement of a small church on Mulberry Street." She delivered the bad news with as little inflection as possible. She knew the idea of going to see a dress rehearsal of an experimental play in the middle of August in the basement of a church on the Lower East Side did not thrill Christopher. She did not tell him that Willie's response to her email question about location indicated he was ambivalent about their coming. Nor did she tell him the working title—"Let's Face It, My Play Isn't Going to Pause the Progress of the Western World"—because if she had, it would have given him everything he needed to pretend to argue against their going—location, heat, and theme. But both she and Christopher knew, no matter what the conditions, he would go for Willie.

"Anyone who can leave the city has already left" were the words he put up in his defense. "No one opens a play in the middle of August."

"It's a rehearsal."

"Even worse. Not even a finished piece. And it will be unbelievably hot and muggy."

But she insisted that heat rises. "It's in the basement. Just don't wear a suit," she called to him in the interval between the sound of their hotel door opening and closing.

She returned to the window. Christopher had said he would be back sometime after five. The day stretched out before her. She wished she had gone with Nick to Calais. She could handle herself. The rain was coming down hard now.

CHAPTER TWENTY-EIGHT

NEW YORK

The theater was small, five rows of ten folding chairs. When Helen and Christopher arrived, all but a few were filled. The audience was a downtown group, proclaimed as much by their black clothing as by their youth. Christopher suspected many were students—former, current, and prospective—of Willie's.

The play started on time. Willie's voice came over the sound system. It was slow and velvety as if he were trying to sell the audience a product. A young woman guided by a flashlight appeared and handed everyone a sleeping mask—the kind given out on transatlantic flights. Willie told them to put on the blindfolds. Once the masks were on, he instructed them to reach underneath their chairs to find a resealable plastic bag, open it, and feel the leaf inside.

Christopher leaned over and whispered to Helen, "Please tell me it's not weed. I have enough to worry about."

She knew he was teasing her, but she also felt splinters of truth in his last sentence.

"You're safe. I think it's only an ivy leaf."

"Feel the veins of the leaf." Willie's voice silked on. "It's the way we retrieve memories. One path leads to the next. It's the connections between the cells. Remembering is not only an act of retrieval but also a creative act of imagination. Each time we remember, connections are being made. If we could draw the act of memory, we would draw a very complex map and one that changes from one act of remembering to the next. With each remembering, we lose control. It's never the same memory twice—just as it's never the same day twice." Afterward neither Helen nor Christopher could connect the ivy leaf prologue with the body of the play except to surmise that perhaps the nonlinear structure tangled with tangents was in some oblique way an enactment of the prologue's metaphor about memory's pathways.

At its most literal, Willie's play was about an artist in a dysfunctional relationship with a woman who was an actress who kept going away. Each time she went away, he remembered her differently, so that the woman who returned was not the same woman he remembered as having left. The play was a succession of departure and arrival scenes. Christopher stopped counting at seven. The play ended with the artist wondering whether it was his girlfriend or his memory that kept changing. The only way he would know for certain that she wasn't changing would be if she stayed. But if she stayed, she, by definition, would have changed. He decided it was impossible to know the answer to his conundrum. The play ended with a line about memory pulling you back and pushing you forward. Helen wanted to ask Willie what he meant by it, but his play had made her feel uncomfortable. She saw a reflection of herself and Christopher. She knew Willie had been working on his play for years. He had told her about it in Saint-Tropez, so she knew he couldn't have based it on them, but she didn't like the way it felt so close. The sense of doom dislodged her from any sense of happiness she had felt being with Christopher in New York.

After the play, Willie, looking as if he had just been pulled out of the East River, appeared onstage to take his bow. Christopher and Helen waited for everyone to leave before going to congratulate him.

"How is your loft coming?" Christopher asked when they were the last three in the basement.

"Well, therein lies a sad tale," Willie groaned and collapsed onto the sofa in his improvised dressing room. "Let's go to dinner tomorrow. I'll make a reservation somewhere close. But first come by for a drink. I need Helen's help on paint colors. I need to find someone who will agree with me."

They heard Willie singing—"Got to find me some thunderstorms and a warm-hearted woman"—on his way to answer the door. He appeared buttoning his shirt. "I probably should have been a country western singer. I think my lyrical talent is underutilized." He had just gotten out of the shower. "Welcome." He kissed Helen on both cheeks. Christopher and Helen stepped over scrap pieces of wood, caulking guns, and boxes of nails as they crossed the room.

Willie asked Helen what she would like to drink. "Nothing for me," she said.

"You are a strange creature."

He fixed Christopher a gin and tonic and then poured some scotch for himself. He handed Christopher his drink and looked at Helen. "You sure?" he asked again.

They walked around the downstairs. Willie amused Helen with the grand names of the paint colors he was considering for the walls—Marie Antoinette Yellow, Sutcliffe Park Green, Della Robbia Red. He explained how he had felt he had a special bond with the contractor. How they had understood each other. "I thought it was okay to give him all the money. Now he's disappeared, and the work isn't finished. The sad thing is that I've spent all summer working on this loft. I had planned to get a lot of writing done, but I've done nothing."

"But you have your play," Christopher said.

"Yes," he said. "But that was written several years ago, and it's still a work in progress." He shuddered the way a dog throws off water. He stood up and offered to finish the house tour. "I'll show you the upstairs. As you can see, it's small and won't take long."

Christopher stood up, too. "Take Helen. You'd like to see it, wouldn't you, darling? I need another drink."

Willie held his drink in one hand as if it were a candle and offered Helen his other. At the top of the stairs, he paused to take a sip. "You know this used to be a belt workshop? I think I can still smell the glue and tannic acid."

She breathed in deeply and paused. "Maybe a little."

He moved to the large industrial window and looked out into the darkness as if trying to see something. "Well, let's face it, we're no longer living in a John Lennon song. Hey, we'd better go downstairs and make sure Christopher isn't drinking all my gin. Also, remind me to show you where I hung the palm trees."

Christopher left for his dinner with Dan O'Connor. Helen stayed and walked to a restaurant with Willie.

Willie ordered after-dinner drinks and made Helen laugh with tales of hardship and duress he endured as a professor of creative writing. "Dying pets—dogs, cats, turtles, goldfish. Dying grandmothers—by the way, always grandmothers and never grandfathers—adolescent boyfriend and girlfriend troubles. The latest is vampires. Now every other story has some vampire angle. The understanding of grammar ranges from severely limited to nonexistent. And if I hear one more time how a story 'flows'—I should just ban that verb from my class. Oh, God, I need more scotch. Where has our waiter gone?"

He walked with her to Broadway and waited until a cab appeared. They talked about Christopher. Willie thought he seemed preoccupied. "I've never seen him so haggard. He's working too hard." Without going into details, she explained that Christopher was spending a lot of time and energy making certain Marc was staying within the tram lines.

As she was getting into the taxi, he said, "You know, if Marc, Christopher, and I were walking down the street, and we saw an automobile turned over with a person trapped underneath, Christopher would immediately run to help, Marc would walk right past it, and I could go either way." She didn't know what to do with his comment and she didn't know why he was telling her this now.

CHAPTER TWENTY-NINE

NEW YORK

"The vast majority of money-laundering schemes are not complex. The biggest hurdle is getting cash into banks, so all you need, really, is one dirty bank." Dan O'Connor laid out an understanding of money laundering and the recent banking regulations adopted to circumvent illegal transactions. Smart as hell and Irish Catholic to the core, Dan had developed a reputation of going after greed and fraud on Wall Street, and Christopher knew he could speak to him in confidence.

Christopher listened as Dan explained how, over recent decades, the laws had tightened. Neither ignorance nor lack of knowledge was an excuse. The Money Laundering Control Act of 1986 established money laundering as a federal crime, and in one of the biggest blows to money laundering—especially the drug cartels—the recent Patriot Act of 2001 prohibited financial institutions from engaging in business with foreign shell companies. While Christopher's jurisdiction was outside the U.S., Dan explained that European countries such as the U.K. either had or were adopting similar, if perhaps not as stringent, laws. The trades Christopher's firm was dealing with were too large to be able to slip into the system unnoticed without the complicity of a bank. Most banks, even if not headquartered in the U.S., had U.S. branches and therefore fell under U.S. banking laws and regulations.

Christopher told Dan that he and a team of tax lawyers and accountants had vetted the trading strategies Marc had devised. Dan's questions and Christopher's answers reassured both of them that the due diligence of the trading activities had been thorough and conclusive. Dan said it made him suspect not the character of the trades but rather the ownership of the funds underlying the trades. He asked if they had examined the entities behind the nominee and corporate names that were used for such trades. He didn't know, but he suspected that Europe was not as strict as the U.S., which, as he had mentioned, had increased disclosure and transparency standards because of 9/11. It became clear to Christopher that when he returned to London he should authorize Nigel and his team to conduct a thorough analysis of the ownership of each account. He wanted to make sure that his firm was holding itself to the highest standard, whether it was required to or not. He wanted to eliminate any possibility of reputational risk.

Dan went on to say that the drug cartels had gotten so powerful and brazen that in a few instances they had backed a "respectable" businessman in his purchase of a small regional bank and used it to wash money. "Their biggest problems are their duffel bags of money. There are a lot of strategies to get the money into banks, such as smurf transactions, in which cash transactions are structured to avoid reporting requirements. But given the size of most of your trades, it would require a small army of smurfs to convert the money into CDs and money orders and then deposit them into banks."

"Smurf transactions?"

"Yeah, named after a cartoon that had all these little blue guys called smurfs running around. In its simplest form, a drug cartel can deposit hundreds of thousands of dollars a day by getting a large group of 'smurfs' to deposit cash in bundles of less than ten thousand dollars but generally around two to three thousand in a number of different bank accounts. It used to be a very successful way to wash money, but since the late 1980s the regulations about suspicious activity have increased. So really about the only practical way to get duffel bags of money into the banking system quickly is through a dirty bank where everyone looks the other way. Once the funds are in the banking system, they can be wired and transferred into European accounts."

"But take the millions of dollars of drugs being sold in the U.S.—doesn't the problem still remain of how to get the cash back into Mexico?" Christopher asked.

"Now they mostly ship it back to Mexico or Colombia in cargo ships and by airdrops. Once the money is 'legitimately' in a Mexican or South American bank, it's traded with foreign banks and financial institutions, so it gets further washed as it moves on."

"Such as Cayman Island securities firms?"

"Used to be that way but not so much anymore. There was so much abuse that there was a big crackdown. Now most of the money—or at least this is what we think—is going to tax havens such as Panama, Luxembourg, Liechtenstein, the Channel Islands, Monaco, and somewhat less Switzerland—only because the U.S. has really pressed Switzerland on its secrecy. But the money launderers are getting more and more sophisticated. There are a couple of brokers who do business with a number of prominent Wall Street bankers."

"Illegal?"

"Well, that's the point. By the time the money gets to them it has been scrubbed so well that it's almost impossible to prove it was ever dirty. They launder money though Europe and then bring it back to Mexico and South America through legal transactions with supposedly lily-white counterparties."

"Such as?"

"Some investment, but trading mostly. For the liquidity. That's where Wall Street comes in. All the major banks have international offices. We've seen a rise in complicated trading strategies such as repos and currency swaps. Those kinds of transactions make the money harder to find than, say, buying and selling corporate bonds."

"Prominent Wall Street bankers? Really?"

"Yeah—there's this one guy, Carlos Muñoz, who specializes in partnerships that own or control monopolies in Mexico." Dan also named six well-known American businessmen.

Christopher recognized all of them, including the name of Charlotte's husband. "Wait. Colson? Eric Colson?" he asked, looking for clarification.

"Yep. He recently made a major investment in a bottling business with Muñoz."

"Surely he's not corrupt?"

Instead of answering, Dan finished his beer and shrugged his shoulders.

CHAPTER THIRTY

NEW YORK

Christopher returned from his dinner more distracted and preoccupied than usual.

"Remember the South American we met at Eastthorpe?" he said, emptying his pockets on the desk in their hotel room.

"Yes, Carlos something—he left early."

"Carlos Muñoz. Turns out he's a very questionable figure. Dan and I were talking about money laundering, and out of the blue he mentioned Carlos Muñoz. He thinks Carlos is some kind of middleman laundering money for Mexican drug cartels."

"Does Marc know this? Why don't you ask Marc?"

"Because I don't know what he knows, but I do know he's not telling me everything. The week I spent in Milan, Marc never once mentioned Carlos's name, and I was with him pretty much every day, all day. A small army of lawyers and accountants didn't find anything either. But we weren't looking specifically for Muñoz or any companies he's associated with."

"If Muñoz is laundering money, wouldn't Marc know?"

"He should. But Dan said all you need is one dirty bank. They take in the funds and don't ask any questions and then start washing it by transferring the funds into different accounts in tax havens like Panama or Liechtenstein or Luxembourg. They use nominee accounts or shell corporations, and soon the trail becomes cold."

"You think Marc is hiding things?"

"I don't know. Dan brought up Eric, who he said had invested with Muñoz in a bottling business in Mexico. He said Muñoz works by attracting equity investors with deep pockets to monopoly situations. Explains why he was invited to Eastthorpe."

"So what are you going to do?"

Christopher rested his front teeth on the top of his thumb and drew in a breath to speak but then stopped himself. Discussing the situation with Helen would not be helpful. She would focus on all the wrong things. "I don't know."

Helen had been looking forward to their flight home, having Christopher all to herself, away from phones and emails. Except for Willie's play, he had worked long hours each day, and she had been alone for most of the week. But on the flight back to London, he was preoccupied and gave her flat, staccato answers. She had noticed that his habit of running ahead of her in conversation—waiting for her to finish so he could get to the point—had gotten worse. He often became impatient, as if she were trying to slow him down. She felt as if he were always trying to redirect her. She compared his situation to Pauling's explanation of converging lines—how where you stand determines what you see.

Christopher laid his newspaper down on his lap to listen. When she had finished speaking, he pushed up in his seat and looked to see who was sitting behind them. No one. "Helen, I'm concerned about corruption, not art." He didn't understand how he had offended her, but he wasn't in a mood to find out.

She knew that once they arrived in London she would feel more desperate. Christopher's driver would be outside their mews house most mornings at six, and he would rarely get home before one A.M. She wasn't like most of the wives of his colleagues and clients—she cared little for money or social connections. No one would ever make the mistake of identifying them as one of the power couples who plotted together to get things done or aimed their attention at those who could advance careers. His absence didn't lend itself to substitution. Going out with friends didn't fill the time. It just made her feel his absence more. She knew she had no ability to affect or influence him. Was that what happened in some marriages, a coming together and then a falling apart? Did children hold couples together? She felt as if they were in free fall with nothing or no one to stop them.

She had no choice but to turn all her attention to work. It wasn't the answer, but it was the best she had. It had been Christopher's idea—though she didn't want to admit this—that she suggest articles she wanted to write—to go after things more. She knew David recognized how good she was and generally gave her what she asked for. She wanted to concentrate on subjects that were grittier and took, as one photographer she had worked with said, a bite out of her soul.

CHAPTER THIRTY-ONE

LONDON

The raid occurred at seven-thirty in the morning. Five officials from the Serious Fraud Office, the SFO, appeared, asked for Christopher, and handed him an inspection mandate. As he read the document, he thought, *Fuck, what has Marc done?* Christopher put them in a conference room, told the official in charge that, of course, he and his firm would cooperate, but he would like to have his counsel present before they assisted with document collection. He stepped outside the conference room and asked the receptionist to get them coffee and tea and to say nothing. He went to his office and called Nigel.

"I'll come over straightaway. See if you can persuade them to delay the beginning of the investigation until I get there. Whatever you do, emphasize your willingness to cooperate. Also, Christopher, get your most senior people to act as shadows for each official. Don't allow them to roam freely around the office. When I get there I'll brief them on what the officials' rights are to search and read documents. They'll probably want to take away servers.

Get the head of your IT department to make certain he has copies of all the files."

While Christopher was speaking to Nigel, Christopher's secretary came in and handed him a note that Marc was holding on line two. He glanced at the message and interrupted Nigel. "Marc just called, he's on the other line."

"Have your secretary tell him you and I are speaking. I'll call him back. You shouldn't. We'll speak about this when I come in. For now just focus on delaying everything until I get there."

When Nigel arrived, he told Christopher he had spoken to Marc. The E.U. Commission had also sent several officials to the Milan office. Nigel had given Marc the same instructions he'd given Christopher and arranged for a partner from his firm's Milan office to assist and advise him. Nigel and Christopher, with the five officials standing by, briefed the seventeen employees who had arrived for the Monday morning meeting. They were instructed to cooperate and warned that they were not to discuss the investigation with anyone outside the firm.

In the privacy of his office, Christopher questioned Nigel about the review conducted earlier in the summer. Nigel told him that he felt they had done a thorough investigation, and the review had been followed with tighter ongoing oversight of the trading options. He said he could not imagine what they could be charged with.

"What are the chances we can keep this out of the press?"

"Zero," Nigel said. "We need to speak to the head of your PR firm—you still use Alan Symons-Smith?"

Christopher nodded.

"We need to bring Alan in. You should meet with him later today, but off-site."

Christopher told his secretary to cancel all his appointments and reschedule them for the following week.

The head SFO official spent five hours questioning Christopher with Nigel present. They asked questions about the founding of the firm, a number of the clients, and the nature of some of the transactions. From what Christopher could tell, a number of the questions were based on information that had appeared in the U.K. and European press. The questions were broad and not difficult. Christopher could not tell where they were headed with the investigation. They did, however, seize the firm's server, his phone, his computer, and the computers of his four most senior colleagues.

By five P.M. the SFO officials were finished for the day and asked to speak to Christopher and the employees. They informed the group that they were coming back the following morning, and nothing could be taken from the premises or destroyed. After they left, Christopher and Nigel reiterated their message. Christopher said that he knew the day had been upsetting for all and that he appreciated everyone's cooperation. He assured them that he and Nigel had recently conducted a thorough review of the business, and as far as they knew, all was in good order. He told them that they might very well get calls from the press that evening, and if so they should decline to comment. He said that he was meeting with the head of their PR firm later that evening, and they would be drafting a response for the press and also for their clients.

They were already an hour late to Louis's birthday party at Annabel's when Helen heard the taxi pull up. For the past two hours, she had been calling Christopher and he had not picked up, so she was angry on at least two counts. She knew Henrietta would be irritated. As he walked in, she stood up. He held up his hands. "Before you say anything—" But she wasn't going to. She knew something was different, and it stunned her.

"Sit down," he commanded her. His voice was not the voice of her husband but that of a man already organizing and assessing his options. He told her about the SFO raid. He explained that they had seized his computer, his phone, and boxes and boxes of files. He couldn't have called her, they would have been listening to everything. He didn't want to tell her over the phone.

"Christopher, you didn't do anything wrong, did you?" She could tell her question wounded him. He looked straight through her as if he did not recognize her.

"No, Helen."

"But then how could this have happened?"

"I have no idea."

He told her she should go on to the party, to make some excuse for him. "There's nothing you can do. Alan Symons-Smith is coming over in an hour. We need to draft a response for the press and our clients."

She didn't want to go. "What should I say about your not being able to make it?"

"I don't know. Just say my flight was delayed."

"I'm not going to lie to my family."

"Okay, Helen, then say whatever you want. But whatever you say, don't get into this with anyone, not even your family. It's very important that you say nothing. Nigel is adamant about this. It won't be helpful."

"How serious is it?"

"Very. But until they charge us with something, it's hard to know. If they do bring charges, and they stick, I could go to jail."

She sat down, dizzy. This world that she found herself in was not of her own making. She had entered it unknowingly—perhaps even unwillingly. A world of high stakes—where greed, betrayal, even bad judgment could destroy a life. It was a world where they had to think of analogies to measure money: twelve days versus thirty-three years. Money held a different place among her friends and colleagues. Money was a stress, not an asset. Her friends and colleagues worried about rent, mortgages, school fees, funds for summer holidays.

He instructed her again to go to Louis's birthday party. "It will seem very strange if we don't show up. It's best to keep things as normal as possible for as long as we can." He believed this, but he also did not want to be distracted by her. She could feel him getting impatient with her. He was already thinking about other things.

As she sat at dinner, surrounded by her family and Louis and Henrietta's closest friends, she watched her brother and sister-in-law. They had a marriage that was organized and orderly. He brought her gifts from his travels, she cheerfully entertained his clients, they celebrated each other's birthdays. They had Leonora and Henry. "How clever," people would say when Henrietta said she had one girl and one boy. Their life together was settled and safe. They did not run through life the way Christopher did. Settled? That was not a word for him. She doubted Louis ever came across any deal, any situation, any person who could put him in jail. How could Christopher not know what his firm was being investigated for? Where did he stand in all of this?

When Helen returned, the door to Christopher's study was shut. She could hear voices of men she did not know. She didn't intrude and went straight to bed. She stayed up until well past the early hours of the next day, and still he hadn't finished. She would speak to him in the morning. But he was up by five thirty and out the door by six.

CHAPTER THIRTY-TWO

LONDON

The on-site investigation finished at the end of the third day. Nigel told Christopher he thought the SFO was focusing on trading activity, although he could not be sure. He based his decision on the devices and documents they had seized both in London and Milan.

When they left the office, Christopher asked Nigel, "What happens now?"

"We wait. There will be more follow-up requests, but that will take place through me."

"What's the worst case?"

"The worst case is that they bring criminal charges, and we start preparing for a trial. Best case is they return the server, the computers, and all the copied files, and we never hear another word from them."

"How often does that happen?"

"In my experience, not often. But the SFO has recently been criticized for not doing more, so this raid could just be some bureaucrat's effort to appear as if he's earning his keep. Marc is pretty high profile, so on one level I'm not surprised."

"Nigel advised me to hire my own lawyer," Christopher said to Helen when he returned home later that evening. He was leaning over unlacing his shoes.

She wasn't sure she had heard him correctly. "He doesn't want to represent you?"

"No, he's representing the firm. It's good advice. He told me who to hire."

"God, Christopher, it sounds really serious."

"It is."

"How long will it last?"

"Hard to say." He repeated what Nigel had told him about what could happen. He tried to be as flat as he could about the situation. No point in getting her upset, especially as she didn't understand securities law or the nuances of what they did. He'd told her he had questioned Marc rigorously, Marc had sworn he had not crossed any line, and Christopher couldn't find a reason not to believe him. He found some sense of comfort in knowing that in the past twelve months, Italian counsel had conducted a thorough investigation of the trading business. Surely Marc wouldn't be stupid enough to do something crazy after that? But he wondered if Marc figured the best time to cross the line was right after the internal investigation had occurred.

Christopher warned her about the articles that were going to appear in the *Telegraph* and *Mail* over the weekend. Despite his PR firm's efforts at damage control, Alan Symons-Smith was clear—the articles were going to be bad. Marc and Ghislaine's flamboyant lifestyle had given the press plenty of material about which to speculate. Marc had courted money that was fast and new, and now the press, who had been waiting for the laws of gravity to engage, were ready to pounce. It was more than an uphill battle. The press was convinced it was impossible to be as successful as Christopher and Marc without being corrupt.

"You should call your parents and brothers and let them know what's coming so they're not blindsided. I should call them myself, but I have to speak to all our employees and clients—we need to get in front of this."

The following morning, David called Helen into his office. "I heard about Christopher's firm. Are you okay? There's pressure to run an article, but apparently Ghislaine is godmother to Christy Farringdon's child—so that may be enough to kill it—at least for now."

Helen didn't say anything, she just listened. She was trying to gather some force around her. She knew Ghislaine and Farringdon's wife were friends, but she didn't know they were close enough for one to be a godparent to the other's child. Had Christopher known any of this and not told her?

"What do you want to do?"

"What do you mean?"

"Do you want to take some time off?"

"No, David, I'd go crazy. I just want to work. I'll do anything."

Helen had tickets for a revival of *Rhinoceros* at the Royal Court Saturday night, and she knew the only reason Christopher agreed to go was that he could get the Sunday papers at the Sloane Square newsstand when the play was over. Their mews house was not far from the Royal Court, and they would usually have walked home after the play, but Christopher hailed a taxi. He opened the papers on the way home. She could tell that he didn't know some of what he read about Marc and Ghislaine. There were several images of Ghislaine with a bright red Birkin bag held in the crook of her arm leaving a Mayfair restaurant, Marc and Ghislaine aboard a Russian billionaire's yacht in the South of France, Marc and Philippe Pavesi in Courchevel. "It reads like a parody of a nouveau riche financier and his trophy wife." He closed the papers and handed them to her.

"I'm going to call Nigel. Don't wait up for me," he said as the taxi stopped outside their house.

Sunday lunch at Willow Brook was worse than Helen expected. She didn't even ask Christopher if he could come. She knew he couldn't. No one brought up the articles that had appeared in the Sunday papers, but she could tell that everyone had read them and probably had spoken at length about them before she arrived.

As the salmon was being served, Helen wanted to shout that no one had died. Instead she made polite chatter with Henrietta about Leonora and Henry. Henrietta said she and Louis were deciding whether to send Henry to Summer Fields or keep him near London. He had a place at Eton, so the question was which school would better prepare him for the entrance exam. Leonora would stay at Francis Holland until she was thirteen and then go on to Wycombe Abbey. Leonora was taking flute lessons, but Henrietta wanted her to take piano lessons, and Louis felt Leonora should choose. Speaking with her sister-in-law reminded Helen of a game she had played as a child—rolling a hoop down a sloped lawn. She would run alongside it, and when it began to wobble, she would brush it forward.

When lunch was over, her father and Louis asked to have a word with her in the library. Helen felt ambushed.

"Your mother and I are concerned about what we have read in the papers," her father began.

Helen didn't react. She had learned from Christopher.

Louis added his concerns. "One has to believe that the SFO would not conduct an investigation if there were not some pretty hard evidence. You should be prepared for that. The papers wouldn't write a story either."

"You're asking me to tell you what I don't know and what Christopher doesn't know."

"Helen, it's his business. It's not as if he's a young associate—he's in charge. It's his responsibility to know what's going on," Louis said.

"I know." She understood her brother's point, she understood he was being protective of her, but she resented his judgment.

She couldn't answer the questions her father and Louis asked, because Christopher had not explained much to her. She realized how little she really knew of her husband's business. He had told her about his meetings, but only in the most superficial way. She was partly to blame, too. She had never been interested in knowing more. He had once said to her that she didn't respect finance or commerce, but it wasn't that—it was more that it had never interested her, and now she wished it had. Despite her absence of knowledge, her father's and brother's preemptive judgments pushed her into Christopher's corner, even though she had doubts it was the right place to be. They had never created anything, had never stuck their necks out, had never taken any risk. Louis and Henrietta lived a safe, predictable life. She felt it was unfair to judge Christopher without knowing more than they did.

"The silver lining is that you don't have children," Louis said. He could tell that he had upset her and quickly added, "I only mean about schools. You know how awful children can be to one another. They overhear their parents talking, and well, they can say mean things to one another. I didn't mean to imply anything else."

As she turned onto the M3 heading back into London, she wasn't so sure Louis had meant that. She felt as if she were trying to investigate a catastrophic crash even before it had occurred. But she had to find the black box, and only Christopher knew where it was.

CHAPTER THIRTY-THREE

LONDON

In the months after the raid, Christopher was so engulfed by the investigation that it was as if he and Helen lived on two different planets. He focused on clients during the day and in the evenings worked late with the law firm he had hired to represent him. After six months, the SFO still had not brought charges, nor had they given any indication of where the investigation was heading. It was hard to know what to prepare for, so he prepared for everything. He and his lawyers reviewed all the firm's transactions—backward and forward—looking for any aspect where a violation could have occurred.

Several months into the investigation, Nigel returned from the Milan office after another full-scale review of the trading operations. Again no improprieties were found. He met with Christopher and filled him in on his findings. Even though Christopher had nothing to do with the trades, he still could be liable. He also knew any charges, let alone convictions, could bring the firm down.

"From what we can tell, everything is in order."

"And none of the trading counterparties have changed?"

"No, still the same big firms—Goldman, Morgan Stanley, Credit Suisse."

"Any with Pavesi and Company?"

"No, Pavesi and Marc are obviously very close, but with the exception of three business development fees, we could find no transactions."

"Is it possible Marc could be keeping some trades off the books?"

"We went through everything with a team of forensic accountants. It's possible Marc was trading through a personal account, but in that case, you're not implicated."

"Then what is my exposure?"

"Well, if everything is aboveboard—and we have no reason to believe it isn't—then you're fine. Worst case under that scenario, the SFO will try to find some infraction—some sloppiness—and slap a fine to save face, but it will only be window dressing."

"How much longer can this go on?"

"God only knows. But the more it goes on without charges being brought, the more pressure on the SFO to close the case."

Christopher could no longer be sure about Marc. His taste for the high life was directly correlated with the amount of time he had lived in Europe. Different countries allowed people the freedom—if not to re-create their background—then at least to hide it. Nuances did not transfer across borders. Marc's desire for residential properties with the correct address, long summer holidays along the Mediterranean coast, winter holidays at European ski resorts, increased each year. He never seemed to have enough. And what, three years ago, Christopher had been prepared to say Marc wouldn't do, he found he could no longer say with any sort of conviction.

After his meeting with Nigel, Christopher left work in time to have dinner with Helen. He wanted to be with her. Over the past months, he had moved away from her. His world of reason and logic, of numbers and legal briefs, had no room for anything that took energy and attention from what he was facing. His concentration had to be intense and absolute. He was not sure she understood, and he wanted her to know. He had missed being with her, missed how her mind was forever tracing latitudes, how she sailed away from words or ideas to find others and then tacked back to find the place she wanted to be.

The early March night was wet and cold. Small patches of leftover rain glimmered like shards of glass on the sidewalk and in dips of pavement. On the walk to the restaurant, he told her only a skeletal version of what Nigel had told him. He wanted to get it out of the way. They could not risk speaking in public places.

They walked to a shoe-box-size restaurant that had just been opened by the owner of a dockside trattoria on the Amalfi Coast, made famous by the number of European yachts that stopped for lunch. As they entered the restaurant, they ran into Fiona and Adrian Campbell—they were just leaving. After they were seated, Helen decided to hang her coat in the hallway outside. As she turned the corner to the coat check, she overhead Adrian saying to Fiona, "Darling, you were awfully cool. You didn't even ask if they were coming to Saint-Tropez this summer."

"Going to jail is more like it."

Helen returned to the table, her coat still in her hands. She told Christopher what she had overheard. It had unnerved her.

"Doesn't it make you angry?"

"Idle chatter." He tried to make her feel better. "Fiona's opinion has no effect on you or me. You expect too much. You expect people to behave the way you think they should." He wouldn't let her know it bothered him, too.

CHAPTER THIRTY-FOUR

CHAMONIX

At the beginning of April, David called Helen into his office and assigned a short article on summer hiking in the Alps. He instructed her to keep the article light for the general reader who wanted something pleasant to consider for a holiday in August. He said he would only print an interview of a guide of happy tourists and not some seasoned mountain climber who railed against the vanities and egos of hedge-fund-fit mountain climbers. "Stay away from controversy" were his last words to her.

Earlier in the week, Nigel had informed Christopher that he had been given an indication that the SFO was finishing up their preliminary investigation. He would soon know if they were going to bring charges. Helen asked Christopher if she should cancel her trip to Chamonix. She wasn't sure he had comprehended where she was going. She suspected she could have said San Francisco or Timbuktu and his reaction would have been the same. By the time she had finished her sentence, his mind was already on other things, calibrating the hours, the days, the weeks before him—performing iterations of scenarios she was incapable of imagining.

"No, you should go. There's nothing to do here. I'm going to be working late every night. We have no idea if and when the SFO will make their decision. There's no point in waiting around."

A week later, she was sitting by herself at an outdoor café along the main street in Chamonix with her notes and various hiking maps spread out in front of her. She had arranged an interview with a professional climber who supported himself by taking wealthy tourists on advanced hikes. He was delayed, but he had called to say he was on his way. She wished he would appear soon. She had given up looking for him in the people who passed—mostly outdoorsy-looking families with one or two young children or shower-deprived, backpack-laden students. Mont Blanc rose behind her, blotting out the sun—a gigantic stone tsunami that oppressed and threatened the town with its shadow. Helen wanted to finish her interview and leave as quickly as she could.

The guide finally arrived. His hair and skin were stained the same color by the sun. The veins in his forearms and calf muscles formed ridges. When he sensed how distracted she was, he did not even try to flirt with her. Besides, he was rattled by what had happened the day before: six dead in an avalanche—two guides and an American family of four.

"It's all about reading the mountain. Climbing isn't the hardest part. Those Americans went up there hoping for the best. That's no way to climb a mountain. You have to be so overprepared that you know you will never fall. Any path can be dangerous. They can all disappear in certain weather conditions. Nothing is guaranteed. All the seasoned guides know how to read the weather and the elements. But it's what they do with that information that matters. The guides get seduced into pleasing their clients. And some of these rich Americans offer bonuses if they succeed in the climb. And it's serious money. My friends with a kid or two find it hard to turn down. They tell me it keeps them from worrying about money, it gives them a cushion in case they want to do something else. But they're never going to do anything else. I tell them not to think that way—that they're perversely taking more risk now that they have a kid. If anything, they should take less risk. But they don't see it that way. You only need one person to make a bad decision for everyone else to follow. They assume if one person goes, then it must be safe."

He shook his head and stirred two packets of sugar into his espresso.

"But the truth is, it's a really big mountain, and most of the people who climb it don't even know or understand what the dangers are. An avalanche doesn't just come out of the blue. We all knew what the conditions were and we've all heard that sound before—the sound of an avalanche coming down the mountain. It gets louder and louder—like a freight train that never stops. The two guides knew they shouldn't have risked it. But their clients had flown all the way from New York, and it was the only time they could all make it, and the father put a lot of pressure on them to go. He wasn't the type who was accustomed to people not doing what he wanted. And those two guides—if they had been honest with themselves and their clients—would have said it wasn't safe to go, but instead they convinced themselves—'Well, just this once, if we're quick we can get up and down.' Whatever they said, they should have known they had said it one too many times." As he spoke, it was as if he were trying to work out the exact equation of how a guided tour could have ended in six deaths.

"And now you have an American family with their two college-age sons dead and two guides leaving behind their wives and three small kids. It's easy to get complacent—no matter how many times you've been up there. Just because you got down safely doesn't mean the odds are in your favor. You have to believe each time you go up, it's a new mountain, and you have to assess the risks as if you've never been up before. Complacency is your enemy. You have to be prepared for the time when your hand slips, you almost have to be expecting it, so nothing can take you by surprise. And you should never go up there unless you know with complete honesty that you're sure it will be okay, because even then there's a chance it won't. And if you go up expecting something or knowing there are odds that something can happen, then you're already doomed. You have to be able and willing to recalibrate when conditions change. It's a belief in yourself that nothing can happen to you, and that belief is only legitimate if you are being honest with yourself. My friends would still be here if they hadn't accepted the money waved in front of them."

Helen kept shifting to thoughts about Christopher and herself as if her mind were a record needle that kept jumping tracks. Maybe the death of his father from an accident that could have been avoided had taught Christopher the lessons the guide now offered. They were embedded deep inside of him. He was prepared for anything. But she was not. Was she not like those Americans who had perished? Had she been too precipitate in marrying him? Had she blindly followed him—hoping for the best? The guide had said, "Any path can be dangerous. They can all disappear in certain weather conditions." It wasn't the investigation that had made things difficult. The difficulty had been there all along. Their love had broken away piece by piece—like the warnings before an avalanche. She had not been careful enough. She had assumed she had to do nothing to protect it. Perhaps she hadn't been prepared for marriage to him. But what did that mean exactly? Maybe as a couple you could only survive if you acted like a climber on a mountain.

As she went through security at the Geneva airport the following morning, she saw Nick van Asten on the other side, threading his belt through his jeans. She hadn't seen him since the day he wrote his number on her wrist. She called his name and was reprimanded by the security guard. Nick heard her and waited for her to come through. He kissed her hello and checked her boarding pass. She had hoped they were on the same flight, but they were headed in opposite directions.

"My flight leaves before yours, but I'll walk with you," he said. He had been visiting his sister in Geneva.

"I didn't know you had a sister."

"Twin, she works as a translator for UNICEF."

They sat down at Helen's gate. She told him about her interview with the professional mountain climber. He took her hand and turned her wrist over. "You should have called me. I would have come and taken pictures for you."

"I don't think you would be in our budget. My guess is they'll use some pretty standard images, probably ones they already have."

"Did you see the series the *Guardian* did on Calais? It could have been ours, with better photos and better writing."

He said he had been asked to replace a BBC photographer who had gotten injured in Afghanistan. He had a week before he was due to meet his group. He was flying to Islamabad and then catching a flight to Quetta where he was meeting up with another photographer and driving north across the border to Kandahar.

"So, Helen, parallel or converging lines—you and me? The way we keep meeting has to be converging, no?"

"You read my article."

"I did. I read all the articles of future collaborators. It was good—the way you refract what's in front of the reader and then turn it at an angle to a larger, more abstract topic."

"I didn't know I did that."

"You do. It's good. No one else does that. I'd like to see what we could do." He checked the screen in front of her gate. His flight was boarding. He took her number and kissed her good-bye. "I'll call you when I'm back."

"Nick," she said, "be safe." He had lost his swagger. She could tell he was apprehensive about what was in front of him. She watched as he jogged through the clusters of travelers until she couldn't see him anymore.

When she handed in her piece, she told David that she had tried to stay away from the controversial topic, but all the guide's comments veered back to the subject as if it were an unavoidable magnetic field. And she thought that readers, given the recent tragedy, would want to know more in order to protect themselves from danger.

CHAPTER THIRTY-FIVE

LONDON

Over the weeks and months, Helen watched him dress in the early morning when it was still dark outside—shirt, socks, trousers, cuff links, shoes, tie, and jacket—the same gestures repeated day after day, week after week, month after month—gestures of normalcy—yet there was nothing normal about where Christopher found himself. He was thinking about the moves in a battle—defections, legal briefs, responses, preparations. He was dealing in an area not his own, so he had to find fluency while still constructing a defense. The only time she had ever seen him look at himself was when he was shaving, and even then he was always looking somewhere else. Not only did he not see himself, he did not see her. She felt as if she had been disappearing little by little over the two years they had been married. She wanted to ask him who he thought he had met three years ago in Bermeja, as a way of confirming who she had been. Could she not remember? Could she have lost so much of herself that she would be unable to recover what she had lost? But they were past the point of conversation. He had no patience for such questions. He would not see the point. All his energy and focus were devoted to defending himself and his firm. She no longer included herself in that equation.

By early spring she noticed that they had received none of the invitations from the prior season—invitations that always came six months in advance. The last time she'd had Sunday lunch with her family, she had gotten angry when Louis told her she was fortunate they didn't have children, the assumption being she would leave Christopher. Did she support him because she believed he had done nothing wrong? Or was she just being stubborn in her refusal to consider he could be guilty? She wasn't even sure herself anymore. Maybe she had been looking at their marriage from the wrong place. But where was the right place to stand? Maybe it had nothing to do with where you were standing but what you were prepared for.

CHAPTER THIRTY-SIX

LONDON

Two weeks after Easter, Christopher returned home shortly after midnight from a meeting with Nigel. Helen, who rarely waited up for him, was sitting in bed flipping through issues of *Country Life*. She still liked to look at the listings of properties for sale in London and in the country, even though she knew they would never be theirs.

"This is unexpected," he said, kissing her and then collapsing in the armchair at the far side of the room.

"I couldn't sleep." She spoke as if picking her words from broken glass. "I just thought it would be nice to wait up for you." She gathered her knees in her arms. She wished he would come over and sit down next to her on the bed.

"I have bad news. The SFO is bringing formal charges." He wrestled with his tie. "Nigel says there's a document detailing a transaction I authorized with Philippe Pavesi that was a sham."

"A sham? What does that mean?"

"I don't know."

"What did Nigel say?"

"He said it has something to do with quote 'a trade lacking market risk.'"

"How?"

"I don't know yet. I rarely got involved with the trading side. When I learned about Philippe and Marc's scheme for the pension funds of Italian companies, I didn't feel comfortable with it and I raised some red flags. We agreed going forward that Marc would get a letter from a top firm, in effect blessing each transaction. And as far as I know, he did that." He shook his head as if to erase what he had said. "So these charges don't make any sense to me. A while back, Philippe brought up a tax straddle idea that had gotten shut down in the U.S. that he thought could work in Europe, but I killed that idea. I don't see how I could be accused of having anything to do with trading or with Philippe. I don't think I've spoken to him in over a year."

"What did Nigel say?"

"He doesn't know. They aren't giving him any sense yet of what they're alleging constitutes fraud."

"When did they say you did this?"

"They aren't being any more specific. I've told you everything I know."

"What can you do?"

"Nothing until we get the charges."

"Why didn't you call me?"

"There's nothing to do. Nigel said I should be very careful about emails and speaking on phones."

"You mean they're bugging your phone?"

"Don't know, but probably."

"But you don't have anything to hide?"

"Of course not—but anything can be taken out of context—misconstrued. It's not worth the risk."

"How bad is it?"

"Very bad. I could go to jail."

"You didn't do it, did you?"

"No, Helen."

"Then how did it happen?"

"I don't know. We're meeting tomorrow morning to go over the evidence the prosecutors have. I can only think that someone in the firm set me up."

"But who could it have been? Do you think it was Marc?"

"I don't know."

"Who else could it have been?"

"I don't know."

"How about your friend Dan?"

"Dan O'Connor?"

"Can't he help you?"

"He would if he could, but he doesn't know the laws and regulations of European markets. He only knows the U.S. This is going to go fast. He wouldn't be able to get up to speed in time."

"God, Christopher, why aren't you furious?"

"I don't have the luxury of being furious."

"Where are you going?"

"To my study."

"Please just come to bed."

"Helen, I have to get out of this situation. I'm the only one who can do it. How can you not understand that?"

CHAPTER THIRTY-SEVEN

LONDON

The trial was set for October. Helen knew Christopher was fighting for his life.

Even when he was talking to her, his mind was always circling, watching for a piece of overlooked evidence, trying to stay ahead of the SFO, trying to anticipate any bad news by finding it first. As she watched him, she had a sense of doom, as if he were preparing for something he would not be able to vanquish. They had lost the ability to make a connection. There was an invisible distance between them. She had allowed herself to believe it was the investigation. When it was over, in what condition would she find her marriage? She would help him in any way she could, but after it was over, she wasn't sure she could find a reason for staying. Hope was beginning to feel foreign.

Within two months of the trial, Christopher and Marc were not speaking to one another. Marc remained in Milan, and Christopher did his best to keep the firm going, but as soon as his competitors learned of the charges, they began picking off clients and associates one at a time. When he came home and told Helen of the latest defection, she would become outraged at the disloyalty, and he would just shrug and say he couldn't blame them. They had families and mortgages. The worst moment came when Jack Greigson, the vice president Christopher had put in charge while he prepared for his trial, was hired away by Eric.

"Charlotte's husband?"

He nodded.

"How can he do that?"

"As you know, a year and a half ago, he was interested in buying our firm. This is a cheaper way of doing it. Our firm is nothing more than people. And he's probably of the view that if he doesn't hire Jack, someone else will."

"But not to come to you and tell you?"

"Yeah, well, this industry isn't known for having choirboys."

"What are you going to do?"

"Call all those who are still at the firm and try to keep them from leaving."

"How are you going to do that?"

He didn't answer. Her questions took up energy and advanced nothing. He didn't have time for any thinking that wasn't strategic. He didn't have the luxury of spending energy and focus on what were, in the end, irrelevant facts. Whether Eric or someone else had hired Jack away, it didn't matter. What mattered was that Jack was leaving. Christopher had to appoint someone to take his place—fast. Most of his senior people had already left. Those who remained were either too junior or just not able enough to keep everything together while he was preparing for his trial.

CHAPTER THIRTY-EIGHT

LONDON

It was as if a bad storm had been barreling toward them with warnings of tidal surges and high winds, and all they could do was prepare and wait. But in the last stretch, it had changed its path and brushed past them, and when it was over, all was left still and swept clean. Christopher got the news from Nigel. The SFO was dropping the charges. All the trades checked out. "They went out on a limb, suspecting they would find a number of sham transactions."

"What about that document—the one detailing the sham transaction I allegedly authorized with Philippe?"

"It certainly wasn't helpful, but there never was a trade. Contemplating an illegal trade—not doing it, well, that's not grounds for conviction. You'll never be able to prove it, but it does look as if Marc or someone closely associated with him was trying to frame you."

"But it doesn't make sense, because you said all along I would be liable for anything illegal Marc did, so in framing me, he would have framed—Jesus, it was a ruse." The suddenness of Christopher's insight made his voice sound brittle.

"What was a ruse?"

"Why didn't I see this before?"

"What? See what?"

"That document. It was a decoy. A diversion. It's so clear now."

"What's clear?"

"What Marc was up to. It all makes sense now."

"What do you mean? All the trades were legal."

"No, not that. He must have anticipated the potential for an investigation. When I first became concerned, I met him in Milan. Philippe laid out an aggressive trading strategy involving tax straddles that he knew I wouldn't approve. It was predicated on breaking the spirit of the law, and I felt the temptation to fix trades would be too great—I didn't want to worry about it. I have to believe that he did that to divert us and possibly the prosecutors, if it ever came to that."

"Sorry, Christopher, I'm not following you."

"The illegal activity wasn't on the trading side. It was never about the trading—the trades were all legal. That's why none of it made sense. It was on the investment side. It's who's behind the names—that's what Marc didn't want us to discover. That document was devised precisely to send the SFO and all of us running down the wrong path—away from Philippe and Muñoz. It's why Muñoz left early from that house party."

"What house party?"

"At Eric Colson's. He was there, but he left early—very abruptly—it didn't make sense."

"You do understand what you're saying?"

"What? That I suspect something illegal? I have all along."

"But the authorities performed a thorough investigation."

"They were looking for the wrong thing."

"It's not your responsibility to show them where they went wrong."

"Fuck, Nigel. Stop speaking in code. You know we can't look away. We've suspected Marc since the beginning, and we looked and couldn't find anything. But that document about the trade—well that's evidence that he panicked. Last summer, Dan O'Connor advised me to look behind the nominee names, he suspected money laundering, but then we were served, so I didn't follow through. But now that I know—or highly suspect—I can't pretend that I don't. Nigel, I don't have a choice. Play it out."

"It's not proven that Marc is laundering money, it's just your intuition. You just went through a thorough investigation by the SFO and you were cleared. If you take this matter further, you will have no choice—there's no turning back. I just want you to understand that. As lawyer to your firm, I would be remiss in not pointing this out. Highly, highly unlikely they are going to come back after you. You could separate your interests from Marc's, which presumably, given the level of distrust and animosity, would be a good thing to do in any event. That way you walk away with half of your firm intact. The other way you lose everything, and possibly, if you are correct, risk charges being brought again. Just go home and talk to Helen and think about it. Take her out to dinner and celebrate. She's been through hell and back, too. Why don't we meet tomorrow morning to discuss this after you've had a chance to sleep on it?"

Both Nigel and Christopher knew that Helen would not be able to pry him from his conviction, but only Christopher perceived that playing it safe was certain to bring about destruction.

CHAPTER THIRTY-NINE

LONDON

Helen flew from her chair and kissed him. "I booked a table at Harry's Bar. Let's drink Bellinis all night. It's finally over."

He took her arms from around his neck and sat down with her on the sofa. "It may not be."

"What do you mean? How could it not be over? You said the SFO had dropped the case."

For the next hour, he explained with more patience than he had shown her in the past year why it was not over, what he suspected Marc of having done. He told her about the implications. All she could think about as he was explaining it to her was Willie's comments about what Christopher would do if he saw someone pinned underneath a car.

Christopher laid out his view, and he laid out Nigel's view, but there was never any question about what he was going to do. She asked him a few questions, a few hypotheticals, but she knew he had already made his decision. She sided with Nigel. Christopher was impatient that she resisted what he was saying. A part of her was ecstatic about the charges being dropped, a part relieved to think he could walk away from his firm, but another part angry that he did not consider her views. Over the time they had been married, she felt as if he had been in a vortex that took all his attention and energy away from her—away from them. Their life had been on hold. Why couldn't he just walk away—didn't she deserve consideration, too? But it was the fact that he had made up his mind before even discussing it with her. Without considering what his actions would mean to her, to them. And her questions were always answered with a form of patient toleration—never a genuine openness to consider an angle she might introduce.

She remembered Christopher's comment about Paolo Pavesi when she had asked him if he thought Paolo loved Bermeja more than his family. He had answered, "But first you have to ask if he is even capable of loving another person. Some people aren't." Had Christopher been speaking about himself? She could only ask that question now, she could not answer it. She had expected a reciprocity to her love that never came. She had waited too long.

CHAPTER FORTY

LONDON

Philip Larkin had been wrong, they would not leave love behind. It was as if they were waiting for something that neither of them would be able to recognize when it arrived. The things that can wreck us—even if we survive—for which, about which, we are given no warning, no ability to be ready, no chance to prepare. A form of neverness.

Helen felt as if she had lost Christopher, but maybe she had never had him. Everyone felt they knew him, but no one did, really. He was impenetrable to her, maybe even to himself. Maybe the mistake she had made was in believing that he could make room for her. But no matter what the errors and omissions, she no longer needed to keep secrets from him, she no longer needed to prove to herself that she didn't need him. She called him at work and said she needed to speak with him, it couldn't wait. Could he meet her at home?

She didn't know what she was going to say or how she was going to say it until she saw him. She told him about finding out she was pregnant and then having a miscarriage. All he could say was "Wait, say that again." She did as he asked.

"You were in Hong Kong. I couldn't wait to tell you, but I didn't want to tell you on the phone, so I thought I would tell you in Morocco, and then you couldn't come—"

"Why didn't you tell me when I saw you?"

"It was too late. When I was in Tangier I felt sick, and when I got back to London, my doctor told me I had miscarried—" She was shaking her head, keeping his words from her. "And you know the pathetic thing? I didn't want to believe him—I even went back the next day to be sure. And you didn't know any of this."

"But how could I have—I wasn't there."

"You never are, that's the whole point. You never will be."

"That's not fair. I don't understand why you didn't tell me about this when I came back."

"I was so mad at you." She was crying as she spoke. "And then I thought I would wait until we were together at Eastthorpe, but then at Eastthorpe you didn't have time for us, you stayed up later than I did, and after that—as pathetic as this sounds—it made me feel stronger keeping secrets from you—to prove to myself I didn't need you."

"Helen, my love, calm down. You don't have to tell me this now."

"Yes, I do. That's the point. It may not be important to you—"

"Of course it's important to me, I just don't want to see you this upset."

"Christopher, this is my life."

"I would have flown home."

"No. No, I don't think you would have. I think a part of me didn't want to even get to that point. To ask that question. I was afraid of what the answer might be."

"What is it you want me to say?"

"I don't know. The fact that you can ask that question after three years of being together—"

"You saw what I was taking on, every step of the way. I feel badly I didn't know what you were going through, but you're being unreasonable."

"God damn it, Christopher, do reason and logic ever not matter to you?"

"Helen, come on. I was trying to keep everything from falling apart. I had to get to the other side. There was no middle ground. You had to have seen that."

"That's the problem. There is no other side. It's a three-ring circus you'll never leave. When this is finally over, you will work even harder to restore what's been lost. It will start all over again."

"Of course it will be hard, but it will be nothing like three years ago, when no one knew me and I had no clients. There will be plenty of young bankers who will send me their résumés. We just had to get clear of all of this."

"I stood by you."

"You're right, you did, but I didn't do anything wrong."

"It's not a question of right or wrong. You don't even seem to recognize how difficult it was being with you. Your world has nothing to do with mine. And I tried to be a part of your world but—God, did I not fit in."

"I never tried to hold you back. I always encouraged you in your work to take on difficult topics—I knew you could handle them."

"That's right, you did. But look where we are now. While your firm was under investigation, you shared very little, and anytime I tried to be helpful you got impatient with me. And now you've made a decision that will affect us both without ever thinking to speak to me, to consider my view. It didn't even cross your mind, and that really hurts. I'm not blaming you, but what's the point? I'll never come first, and I wasn't expecting to be first all of the time, just once in a while. It makes me feel pathetic. I just don't like who I've become being with you."

When she told him she was leaving, she interpreted his silence as not caring enough to fight back. And yet despite all that had happened, she would have given anything for him to have said, "Helen, don't go." She had carried hopes and dreams and expectations around with her. "Sometimes when I waited up for you, I'd fall asleep with images that took me to faraway places—as if they were a pillow against which to lay my head. But I don't have them anymore. They've disintegrated, and when I look for them, I can't find them."

He listened and said nothing. It was as if he had lost his voice. He recognized everything she said. He didn't try to hold her back. He knew she thought he had been making a choice when he hadn't been. He had passed the point of inflection, and now nothing could surprise him. There had been only one way out of the trouble he was in, and he had not been willing to trust anyone but himself to get himself out. Over the months, he had reviewed everything his firm had done, had learned U.K. and E.U. securities law, read cases and opinions, had trusted she would wait. But he had watched as she had grown more distant, as if she were trying out what she had already decided. He had done nothing about it.

It is the rare person who can describe seeing something unfolding before anyone else. That's not to say they understand it, just that they see it happening. He understood it was over. But when she walked out the door, he felt as if his skin were being torn off his body. At that moment, hope was not a thing he wanted. He had always taken refuge in things—numbers, spreadsheets, analytics—no emotions, no angst, no disappointments—just cold, hard, inanimate objects and symbols. For a long time he had felt as if he had been holding walls from collapsing and he had nothing left to offer her. He couldn't tell her he was sorry and that he would try harder, because he knew that wasn't at the heart of it.

CHAPTER FORTY-ONE

LONDON

The week Helen left, Christopher arranged to speak to Dan O'Connor. While he did not know U.K. law, Dan told Christopher that if he were his client in the U.S., he would advise him not to go to the authorities.

"Don't be naive. In the real world, prosecutors aren't all good guys. In fact, many of them aren't. One of the reasons I decided to go into the private sector was that too many of my fellow prosecutors were just looking for heads. Most of them have political ambitions. In fact, that's why a lot of them become prosecutors in the first place. For them, reasons one through nine are about headlines—truth and justice a distance tenth.

"If your partner is clever at spinning his own version, you're putting yourself at risk personally in pursuit of a conceptual idea. You'll be getting yourself into a street fight with the mafia—some of whom call themselves prosecutors, some of whom call themselves partners. And in a street fight—with two from the mafia and one from the Boy Scouts—who do you think is going to win? And listen, if Muñoz is involved, I'd bet my last nickel there are grounds somewhere for criminal charges. You should stay as far away from all this as you can. It's a corrupt world. The risk-reward isn't worth it. For what? To prove a point and send your partner to jail?

"It's not about truth and justice, it's about protecting yourself and your family from a system that is unpredictable. You have to do what's in your narrow self-interest. Do you want your fate in the hands of twelve strangers? Think about it. And Christopher, I don't know about the SFO, but if the U.S. Attorney's Office had looked into a firm and found nothing, and the firm either ceased business or split up, the chances of us going back to investigate are zero to none. Remember, these guys want high profiles and big headlines. Even if Marc has done some illegal things, they can't have been so big or they wouldn't have been missed the first time."

Christopher understood that Nigel and Dan were giving him their best advice, and he understood the rationale behind their thinking. He knew each side of the equation, but he also knew what Marc had done, and even though he knew they were ending their association, he wanted to have no part of the illegal activity. Going to the authorities was the only way he could be certain of that.

Christopher confirmed his decision to Nigel, but first he was going to tell Marc what he was going to do. Nigel was clear. "It's a lunatic's move." Christopher didn't owe Marc anything. Furthermore, the SFO would most likely instruct him to wear a wire.

"I'm not doing that."

"It's the only way to protect yourself."

"Yeah, well, I'm not going to do it. Marc isn't going to say anything to me anyway. I had nothing to do with what he was up to. There's no evidence. I'll take my chances."

Marc was in Paris. Christopher flew the following day and met him in the bar at the George V. Marc was sitting at a table in the far back. He was tanned, he had just gotten back from Il Pellicano. Christopher could tell he was expecting to celebrate.

Christopher explained what he had figured out.

"I don't know what you're talking about. But what does it matter? It's over." Marc raised his glass of champagne.

"I'm going to the authorities to lay out my suspicions, just as I'm laying them out now. Consider this a dress rehearsal."

Marc scrutinized Christopher with dark, impenetrable eyes. Hatred and animosity transformed his face. "You're a fucking idiot." He stood up, tossed two hundred-Euro notes on the table, pushed past Christopher, and left, neither wanting nor waiting for a response.

Christopher wasn't surprised by Marc's reaction. He had expected all artifice to disappear. He also knew that by telling Marc what he was going to do, he was giving him a head start.

The following day, Christopher went to the authorities. After another three months of investigations, the SFO confirmed that Philippe Pavesi was implicated in a money-laundering scheme that involved dirty money being brought to a Mexican bank controlled by Muñoz. The dirty funds were then transferred to nominee names in Liechtenstein accounts controlled by Philippe and invested in various funds and instruments devised by Marc. When and what Marc knew, the SFO could never be sure. The SFO did not have enough evidence to convict him personally. Marc had been clever enough or lucky enough to escape individual prosecution. Nigel said he had never seen one so accomplished at staying in the gray zone. The one thing Christopher was sure of was that Marc had panicked. The false document implicating him was proof.

After the investigation and the resulting settlement and fines, Christopher had very little of his firm left to salvage. He could start over, but he knew what it took to build a business. His colleagues and clients had witnessed the betrayal, and they had admired the way he had acted when everything was on the brink. They now urged him to consider restarting his business, throwing his shoulder against it one more time, but he didn't have it in him. He spent the last week seeing his clients, explaining what had happened. Thoughts of the future were not yet in front of him. And now that it was all finally over, he would take some time to think about what he would do next.

Christopher assembled a small team of accountants and lawyers to unwind the remaining pieces of the business. He found good positions for his few remaining employees and negotiated the sale of the assets management business to a small U.K. bank. He got what he could for the lease of the Black Friars Lane office. Helen had once told him that she felt he could pack up his life in minutes. She was wrong, but he understood why she had said that. When he locked the office door for the last time, he thought how all those decisions and all those hours were crumpled and discarded with a 180-degree turn of a key.

While the investigation was going on, his mother had decided to move from Fontainebleau to an apartment in Paris. Her manager had quit and she needed help closing up her farm. She had more horses than she could handle. Laure was seven months pregnant and confined to bed rest, so Christopher complied.

We have to break ourselves apart sometimes, Christopher thought as he drove to Fontainebleau. Somewhere along the way he had tried to make himself immune from disappointment. He had spent so much of his energy keeping everything shut, battened down, not throwing any part of himself open. Not looking back was something so well practiced that it was, by now, a reflex. It was the only way he had known how to protect himself. But it had not worked.

As he drove through the town to his mother's property, he thought, *Destruction comes about in such a clear and fast way.* He knew his marriage was over. He had not been willing or able to give Helen what she wanted or needed. Had he subconsciously been trying to push her away? Maybe in the end that was what had made her leave. In the middle of the night he reached for her and knew she was not coming back.

CHAPTER FORTY-TWO

LONDON

Helen stayed away from her family and any friends wanting to give advice. She returned to her small top-floor flat on Old Church Place in Chelsea. She had forgotten how much she loved the cool light that came in from its north-facing windows. She put most of her things in storage to avoid any traces of Christopher. Once a week, she had dinner with Peregrine to help push his work along. Peregrine had little understanding of relationships, so the topic of Helen and Christopher never came up. She knew the best thing for her to do was to keep her head down and write as many articles as David would allow. As the summer months approached and work began to slow down, Helen walked into David's office and said she wanted to go as far away from London as she could. David covered his face with his hand. "Okay, but hopefully it's not another prima ballerina in search of the letter 'J'?"

"That story was successful. We received a lot of—"

"You're right. I remembered that as soon as I said it. How about a travel piece? Do you still have an interest in going to Cuba?"

She explained her idea about a circus performer who had traveled around Cuba in the 1850s. She could use a few of the passages from the memoir as a way into the article. She recognized only a few of the many cities where Glenroy had performed—Matanzas, Espiritu Santo, Santiago de Cuba, Manzanillo, Santa Cruz, Santa Clara—but from what she had read, she could tell that Cuban life had been grand and gracious. An article about Cuba a hundred and fifty years ago could be intriguing, especially if she were able to track down the descendants of the Marquis de Cardenas.

David lowered his glasses to look at her clearly. "Just to make sure I understand. You want me to send you to Cuba not to write a travel piece on Havana but to write about a circus performer—an American one at that—who lived over a hundred and fifty years ago."

"It's not a crazy idea."

"Okay, I'm listening."

Helen did her best to convince him, but the story did not move him. He reminded her that their readership would only be interested in Havana and not in the list of towns she had rattled off, which he had never heard of. He had no idea how she could spin her idea into an article, but in the past when he had given her leeway, she had surprised and impressed him. She couldn't give him a strongly reasoned understanding of what the piece could end up being except to say she would begin by tracing the travels of the circus performer. They both knew that some of her best work came from going places when she did not know why she was going there. Plus, he knew she and Christopher were having a difficult time, and he sensed it was important for her to go. He hoped it was just one of those bad patches every marriage goes through.

Helen couldn't define why she was so fascinated with the story. Perhaps she felt some deep sense of concern for this little boy who had learned to navigate an unsympathetic world by himself at an early age. She sensed he had found refuge in Cuba and she wanted to try to unravel why. His account was so lacking in emotion, and yet he said his purpose in writing was to give pleasure to others. "And now readers farewell, hoping that a recital of my slight experiences expressed in the foregoing language have allowed you to pass a few pleasant hours." Was it because he had led such a solitary life that he felt the need to share it with others? Maybe she was searching for the words that had not been written, trying to find a key to his flatness, his lack of emotion, trying to understand what was underneath. Could her desire to understand be related to her failure to understand Christopher? Did it matter anymore?

CHAPTER FORTY-THREE

HAVANA

Havana was not a city to visit alone—at least not the first time. Had Helen been with Christopher, she would have liked to think they would have spent all afternoon and evening walking around the civilized ruin of a city that once had tried to rival Paris and Madrid in its grandeur. They would have paused to have a coffee or a glass of wine or a cold beer at one of the outdoor cafés, and she would have made up stories about the tourists who strolled by. They would have gone to dinner each evening at different *paladares* in the old section of the city.

Through a contact at the paper, Helen was introduced to a young American couple, both journalists, who had moved from Brooklyn to Havana to write novels. He was of Cuban descent, and they had been offered his uncle's house for a meager under-the-table rent. They had a small child, and he had just published a children's book about baseball. Helen explained her idea to them over a supper of beans and rice and cold beer. She asked about the Marquis de Cardenas. They had never heard of him. They said it would be impossible for her to get access to the National Archives, but they did tell her about the man who had the official title of city historian of Havana. He might be able to help. They advised her to stop by his office the following morning to make an appointment.

She showed them her map. They had not been to any of the towns. They said they had to be careful not to do anything that suggested they were still journalists. They did not have a car, and gas was not easy to get even if they did have one. The only town they commented on was Santa Clara, a town in the middle of the country, the site of Che Guevara's last battle with Batista's forces. But that was not why they mentioned it. They had heard about a bishop who kept a low profile but was pushing the government in civic areas. He had amassed a large library of printed material and archives and provided a cool, well-lit space for students to study in the evening. They couldn't remember his name, but they told her Santa Clara was small, and his diocese would be easy to find. It was close to the town square. Her hotel would be able to arrange a guide to take her. "Be careful," they said. "Anyone in the travel services works for the government as a spy. Tell the guide you want to go to Santa Clara to see the site of Che Guevara's victory, and then, when you are there, you can 'stumble' across the bishop."

On her way to the office of the city historian, Helen walked along the Malecón. The waves were hitting the rocks at the base of the concrete sea wall and bouncing back, sounding like echoes of the wind. The historian's office was in a two-story house built around a courtyard. Louvered shutters kept the interior-facing loggias shaded from the sun. His assistant said he had meetings all morning and taught in the afternoon. The earliest he could see her was the following morning.

She spent the afternoon walking around the old town. She liked coming to countries where she was not facile with the language. She could hear herself breathe in these places. The coming and going of motorized bicycles ricocheted down the narrow alleyways of three- and four-story houses. A woman gave a rug, draped over her balcony, hard slaps with a stick. Helen wandered past the Catedral de San Cristóbal but did not go in. She found a café and ordered a coffee. She watched flocks of tourists drift around the city. She noticed a group of three women, all dressed in white, followers, she assumed, of the Santería religion. They crossed the plaza and headed down an alleyway behind the cathedral.

She returned to the small hotel where she was staying and tried to take a nap before the late evening meal. Her room was at the back of the building and was hot. She opened the window, but the sound of voices and metal bins being moved below shattered the quiet in irregular intervals. Despite the hotel's assurances, there was no internet. She typed her notes and then headed back outside to the Malecón.

The wind had quieted down and was no longer crashing waves against the sea wall. She watched the seagulls and pelicans and tried to decipher the algorithms of their movement. Two men in a small rowboat headed out to sea as if making their getaway. She walked along and looked at the people passing her. Most were in groups of two, men with wives, boys with girlfriends. An old lady sat on the wall knitting a pair of baby booties and looking out over the sea. She was passed by a young man with a gym-built body who offered his shirtless chest to the sun. A middle-aged woman stopped to look in slow motion for things that could not be found in the sea. Who were these people? A cluster of small children shrieked and shrilled as if imitating happy seagulls. She thought about her nieces and nephews. Henry, who was turning eight, would be going off to Summer Fields in September.

The afternoon felt old.

She had wanted to go to a place she had never been with him. She had wanted to go to a place where no one would know who she was, a place that could protect her from the three and a half years she had lived with him. In the evening, she walked down to the harbor before dinner. She looked out over the sea. There was nothing to do anymore. Time was stretching out. Everything was as empty as the flat surface of the water.

She watched the people who came to dinner at the restaurant. The Russian couple who started with mojitos and ordered lobster and who did not say one word to one another. She couldn't decide whether they were bored or just comfortable and food and drink were their main pleasures. Then there was the Canadian couple—he was tanned but unathletic looking, a little heavy, and wore glasses that were severe and angular and suggested he might be an architect or a designer. His wife had gotten a lot of sun, and her shoulder-length hair was blond and still wet from a shower. She was thin and fit and refused all attempts by the waiter to give her a second helping of the fricase de pollo they had ordered.

Nights were the hardest. She listened to the sound of the cars until the intervals between them stretched past each hour. The space between two thirty and four was the quietest. Once in a while the clank of a bicycle or a motorbike heading home restarted the interval of silence. Just after five, the air filled with sounds of people heading off to early morning jobs.

The city historian knew nothing about the circus that had traveled the country in the 1850s and doubted that there would be any information in the National Library. Nor was he interested in learning more. He only wanted to speak about his work in Old Havana, how many buildings he had restored and how many more he planned to save. Halfway through the interview she understood that, because she spoke English, he had assumed she was American. When she corrected his understanding, he seemed to relax but also to lose interest in telling her about the funds needed to continue his projects.

She asked about the Marquis de Cardenas, he proceeded to tell her about the town of Cardenas, and she was not sure if he understood her question or only offered what he knew. She asked again about the marquis, who had given Glenroy refuge at one point. He didn't know anything about the marquis, but he did know the house that had belonged to the Cardenas family in the 1800s. He spoke very excitedly about the Casa de la Obra Pía. The Cardenas family had inherited the beautiful home of the Obra Pía Charity. He couldn't tell her when. The house was now a museum, and she could walk there—it was not far from his office. As his cordial way of ending the meeting, he stood up and pointed to the painting hung behind his desk. It was of a road that disappeared into a forest. He told her that he liked the image because he understood that there was never an end to his projects, and he always started them off without knowing how he was going to finish them. "Things are there whether we see them or not. The path is there, we know it continues, we just can't see where, but we know it continues." He walked out with her and pointed in the direction of the Casa de la Obra Pía.

The docent of the museum knew even less than the city historian. If she were not more successful, Helen knew that at some point soon she would have to let go of what she was trying to find. She returned to her hotel and asked the manager if he could arrange a driver to take her to Santa Clara. She said she wanted to see the sight of Che Guevara's famous battle. The manager told her she looked tired. She asked to have a tray brought to her room for dinner.

CHAPTER FORTY-FOUR

SANTA CLARA

They left at seven and followed a two-lane road out of Havana. They drove through communities where small one-story houses were clustered around railroad crossings, where skinny, worn-out horses pulled buggies past small farms, where a goat or cow was kept enclosed by densely planted cactuses trimmed in straight lines, where people with leathery skin and clothes that had been washed and laundered for decades walked slowly. The car was old and they drove with all the windows down. Villages became clusters of houses, small clusters of houses became fields, fields blurred into borderless stretches of land long left untended.

The driver turned south, and soon there were only acres and acres of orange groves on both sides of the road—no houses, no cars, no farm equipment. Only once did Helen see a man. He was on an ill-nourished horse moving in a slow jog down a row of trees. A thin dog followed a safe distance behind. She didn't know if the man was overseeing the groves or just passing through. Soon, in the distance, she saw a long four-story building rising out of the field.

It was gray concrete that had never been painted and looked as if construction had been abandoned at some point. She tapped the driver's shoulder and asked about the building.

"Dormitories."

"All the way out here? For what?"

He explained that during the 1970s and 1980s, the USSR had invested in Cuban industry and agriculture. They had built the dormitories for students who were required to work the fields planting orange trees for five days every other week.

"All the students?"

"All the students."

"But what if you didn't want to plant?"

The driver shrugged. She suspected he had been one of those students, but he did not volunteer the information and she did not ask. She remembered what the American couple had said at dinner about drivers being spies.

"And now?"

"After the breakup of the USSR, the program was abandoned. No one comes. Everyone wants to be in Havana. Money is much better."

She wanted to stop and look at the building, but they had passed it, and she knew if she were too inquisitive early on, she might unnerve him and sabotage her plans to find the bishop.

As they were about to turn onto the National Highway, which ran the length of Cuba on an east-west axis, they were overtaken by a large tour bus. It was Chinese made and filled with Japanese tourists, the driver said. They were heading to the alligator farms on the western tip of the island.

From the map in her guidebook, Helen guessed they would be in Santa Clara in an hour. They were making good time on the road, which looked more like a boulevard in a European city abandoned in the 1950s than a national highway—four lanes with a grass median separating the two directions and ornate black lampposts appearing at random intervals. There were no signs anywhere. On either side, invasive *marabu* trees had taken over large swaths of land. Considered a weed in Cuba, the thorny trees grew in dense thickets and in some areas reached heights over twenty feet. She had read somewhere that Cuba imported most of its food, which surprised her now, seeing how rich the land was. They drove east for over an hour, and she counted four trucks and three cars. There was something soothing about the sameness of the land skimming past.

As they turned off the highway, the driver told her there was a famous cigar factory she might like to see in Santa Clara. She was happy to stay away from any of the tourist spots, but he was insistent, and she sensed she should not resist.

The cigar factory was several blocks from the center of town and smaller than Helen had imagined. The streets leading from the town square were narrow, with more horses and buggies than cars. The factory was the width of one of the buildings—not more than forty feet wide and extending deep into the block. Inside were rows and rows of tables where workers—mainly women but some men—sat with piles of tobacco leaves. She watched as their hands moved across the five piles, choosing a leaf for the wrapper from one pile, three for the filling from three separate piles, and then one for the binder from the last. Their fingers moved with so much memory that they seemed detached from their bodies—as if they had a heartbeat of their own.

She soon understood why the driver had been so keen to take her to the factory. His mother worked there. He had surprised her by coming. Even after they embraced, she clasped his face in her hands and did not want to let him go. Helen noticed a man in a small enclosed cubicle that had been built out from one of the walls. When her driver joined her, she asked why they needed a security guard.

"Oh, he is not security. He is the reader. He reads to all the workers. In the morning he reads the news, in the middle of the day, stories of general interest, and in the afternoon, novels—tales of love and romance." These middle-aged women—all day on a bench rolling cigars, an extended motion performed more times than the times they brushed their children's hair or leaned over to help with homework or cooked the evening meal—were joined together by this one man, who came every day and opened the world for them with words. She walked by the reader's cubicle and saw a thick paperback on his desk with a faded cover and curled pages. *Lil, la de los ojos color del tiempo* by Guy Chantepleure. The pen name made her smile—it had to be a woman, French most likely, who had probably written before the revolution. Everything in Cuba dated back to some time before the revolution. She wrote down the name of the novel though it would not be hard to remember—and the idea that time had eyes reminded her of the end-of-year party in Bermeja when the poet recited Baudelaire's poem about the moon. When she returned to London, she would try to locate a copy. She liked the idea that she would be reading the same text as the workers.

The driver kissed his mother good-bye. She was slow getting back to her workstation. Even after she sat back down and continued rolling cigars, she kept smiling at him. Inspired by the admiration from his mother and her fellow workers, Helen's driver assumed a more official air and informed her he would now give her a tour of Santa Clara. They walked to the town square, but the heat and his homesickness wilted his ambition. When she suggested she might walk around a bit and meet him in an hour, he was happy to oblige her. They agreed to meet in front of the tallest building in the square, the Santa Clara Libre, formerly the Santa Clara Hilton. He headed back to his mother.

From where she stood, she identified a tall spire and walked toward it. The well-maintained church and the two flanking buildings stood out like an oasis amid the decay. Helen knocked on the door and a nun answered. Helen explained who she was and her reason for coming. She pulled out her copy of Glenroy's book and explained that he had performed in Santa Clara in the 1850s. She had heard that the bishop had amassed a large library of periodicals and newspapers and wondered if he might have some historical information on this circus. She said they most likely had performed in the square.

The nun, who spoke very little English, did her best to navigate what Helen was trying to tell her, but Helen wasn't sure how much she understood. She explained that she would be in Cuba for the next two weeks and would like to come back to see the bishop. She left a handwritten note for him, telling him she would telephone the next day to see if they could find a time to meet. Maybe the bishop could be the subject of an article—a story about a holy man creating a community center for the youth of his town, a place where they could study in the evening. She wanted to understand how he worked with the government, given that Castro had expropriated much of the Catholic Church's land when he came into power. As she walked back to the square, she was struck by the absurdity of what she was trying to do. Here she was, in a country where she couldn't speak the language, trying to see a bishop who probably wouldn't see her because he was fearful of her being either an agent of the government or a misguided journalist who could bring the unwelcome attention of the government to his good work.

She met the driver at the agreed time in front of the rundown hotel. He resumed his position of guide and pointed to the pockmarks made by bullets on the faded mint-green–stucco facade. The hotel had been the scene of one of the last gunfights of the revolution. It had not been touched since then.

They turned back onto the National Highway and sped toward a sun that would not give up its heat as it descended. They passed a teenage boy standing by the side of the road who looked at them with hope as they passed. She looked back at him. The driver explained the boy was selling bars of homemade nougat, she asked if they could stop. No, he said, it was illegal, but he could not explain why. She leaned her head against the door, hoping to shut her eyes and take a nap, but the unexpected jolts from the worn-out highway and stripped-out car sabotaged her plans and kept her awake. They traveled alone, neither passing nor being passed.

As they turned onto the secondary road, the cool air scented with orange trees refreshed her, and she sat up and watched for the building placed so incongruously in the middle of the groves. The driver confirmed they were returning the same way they had come. When she saw it in the distance, she asked him if they could stop. He waivered, but she countered by saying, "For only ten minutes." They were getting back later than expected; it would be dark soon, and his boss would not be pleased; but he was grateful for having been able to spend time with his mother, and he had already refused her once, so he acquiesced.

He slowed and turned down the narrow dirt road. High weeds ran down the middle. The car bucked across the deep ruts. As they approached, the gray concrete building rose slowly as if a gigantic door leading to a world on the other side of the water-colored evening sky. One strand of barbed-wire fence delineated the property boundaries, which included a half-acre grove of mango trees. As they turned toward the building, the driver turned on his lights. Sitting on the steps in front of the building was a couple who moved away from the cones of light. As the car settled to a stop, the man, in torn shorts and a thin tank top, approached. The driver explained that Helen had wanted to take a look. The woman came out of the shadows. She was wearing a soiled pair of tracksuit bottoms and a T-shirt. She smiled and stayed at a distance. A thin black cat crouched on the steps of the building and then darted off.

The man and woman lived in a small apartment on the ground floor. Their job was to keep people from vandalizing the building—not that there was much to steal—copper wiring perhaps. They had no electricity so they spent the evenings sitting outside until the light disappeared. It had been a school and dormitory for students, the man explained. He asked the driver if they wanted to see the building. Helen understood enough to nod her head before her driver could decline. The man led them up a wide set of stairs in the middle of the building. The open staircase was lit by the last slivers of daylight. On the third floor he showed them a large empty room. He explained that the room was the dormitory for the boys. On the other side of the building was the dormitory for the girls. The driver had already started back down the stairs by the time the man was showing her where the boys had written their names—Enrique, Mario, Francisco, Luis, César, Victor, Antonio, Armando, Cuarto—all written by different hands. She asked if anyone ever came back. He shook his head. "*Nunca*."

The woman was standing outside with a small plastic bag when they stepped out of the building. She handed the bag to Helen. Inside were mangoes she had picked. Helen assumed the woman was the man's wife. They were isolated in the miles and miles of orange groves. They did not have a car. They would have a long walk to get supplies. Maybe someone dropped them off. She wondered if they got lonely or if being with each other was enough. Just the two of them, as if isolated on a tiny island. Maybe being with another person so completely could make any condition bearable. The way she leaned against him made Helen feel alone. When she turned back to wave good-bye, it was too dark to see them.

The roads were narrow and rough, and Helen had no sense of which direction they were traveling. In the darkness, there was nothing to orient—no lights, no road signs. She remembered reading that in order to get a license, a pilot had to learn to fly only by his instrument panel because in the darkness it was so easy to become disoriented. She could understand that sense of disorientation even without being airborne. When they came to a crossroad, the driver knew whether to turn left or right or continue on.

The feeling of disorientation felt familiar—that's how it had been with Christopher. She remembered part of a conversation. She didn't know why it had come back now. She remembered something he had said to her: "When I first met you, I knew we could have some real surprises. I didn't know what was going to happen, but I was sure things would happen that I didn't expect." "Good things?" "Yes, good things."

She was beginning to think she would not find enough to write about Glenroy and the circus. She began to wonder what she had thought she could find. At some point she should stop trying so hard and let the story find her. She would call David in the morning and speak to him. She was not sure a story about the bishop would appeal to him—she was not sure the bishop would cooperate. The nun she had spoken to was guarded, and she knew they had to be concerned about any article appearing in the Western press. She sensed the government was allowing the bishop to operate as long as he kept things under the radar, but any sort of profile could cause them to rein in the freedom he had been allowed.

They arrived back in Havana just after ten P.M. The driver turned into the fringes of the old city, there were no streetlights, and all the houses were dark. Very few houses had electricity after nine o'clock. It had rained while they had been away. She would later remember how the puddles of water on the uneven streets reflected only the light of the moon and made it seem much later than it was. As they pulled up to her hotel, she handed the driver the bag of mangoes. "For your children."

CHAPTER FORTY-FIVE

HAVANA

The sound somersaulted toward her. It would not go away. It insisted its way into meaning. She reached toward it.

"Helen."

What was this world? Where was she?

"Helen. It's Christopher." His voice steadied and confused her.

"Christopher." She had not spoken to him in several months—not since their split—but saying his name again had the odd and unexpected effect of anchoring her in the darkness. She turned the alarm clock toward her. Four A.M. Why was he calling? She sat up and held her head to find her balance. The stone floor was cold.

"Are you with someone?" His question made her know that he had given up all claims on her. And in that moment, she understood how words were likes pieces of cloth with threads from past feelings and desires woven through them.

"Where are you? Are you here?"

"I'm in Fontainebleau. I'm sorry to wake you. I've been trying to reach you for several days. I've emailed and left messages on your phone."

"Yeah, no, I'm in Havana. There's no internet, and my phone doesn't work here." She was still trying to locate the day that was about to begin.

"I called your office and David gave me this number—where you're staying. He said he wasn't certain when you would be back."

She knew where she was now. The remaining fragments of confusion had settled down around her. She looked out the window. Dawn was nowhere in sight. It would be another two hours before people appeared riding bikes to work along the Malecón.

"There are just some papers you need to sign. I'm putting the mews house in your name." It was the way his voice closed around the words—as if something fragile had been hidden away all these years—a fragment of a feeling that, if exposed to the elements, would disintegrate.

"I don't want it."

"You can sell it."

"Can't everything wait until I get back?"

"Yes, it can. I just have to let my lawyer know. I'm leaving today for a while."

"I'm back in two weeks."

"Okay, I'll let him know."

"Christopher, where are you going?"

"Bermeja."

CHAPTER FORTY-SIX

BERMEJA

When Helen hung up the phone, she knew her heart would never have full clearance from him. She understood that she had been searching for the wrong person. It was not Glenroy she had been trying to find, but Christopher. She waited for the concierge's office to open ahead of other guests exchanging money or complaining about the lack of phone service in their rooms. Without internet or the ability to make long-distance calls, she needed help changing her flight. The concierge told her it was impossible to change her ticket—she would have to buy a new one. There was a flight leaving Havana the next morning at six A.M., connecting through Mexico City to Manzanillo with a nine-hour layover. She agreed and paid cash because she had no choice. She had eighty pounds left, but she would have time to find an ATM at the airport in Mexico City.

She was at the José Martí International Airport by four thirty A.M. Her flight was delayed and did not take off until ten forty-five A.M. She would still have a little over four hours to make her connection. When she arrived in Mexico City, she went to the British Airways lounge to check and answer emails. Three from Christopher over the past week. She read and reread them, looking for signs, but they were basic, factual, unemotional. They all said the same thing—he was putting their mews house in her name and she would have to sign some documents. There was no information about when he would be traveling to Bermeja or how long he would stay. She was oddly relieved. It was better to have no answer than the wrong one. She also knew she could send him an email telling him she wanted to come see him, but she did not want to be wrong about her decision or about him.

The distance from the small landing strip to Casa Tortuga was a little over two miles. Christopher had not arranged for anyone to collect him. After months and months in offices and conference rooms, the thought of being able to walk up a hill with views of the Pacific Ocean over his left shoulder, with nothing to do and no one to see—felt luxurious. To come to a place where life spooled out measured and marked—where the sun rose in a slow and steady way and shadows spilled across the land dictated by unbreakable laws of physics—felt necessary.

He stopped to watch the small prop plane hurrying back to Puerto Vallarta. He remembered the first time he had seen it. He had watched it dip its wings to the fishing boats below. On such a small stretch of land, the pilot, the fishermen, and the farmers would all know one another. Very likely they were all related by blood or marriage. But today the pilot was in a rush—he had refueled quickly, no time for a coffee and chat at the landing strip. He was worried about the weather. An approaching storm had chased all the fishing boats back to shore. Most of the summer days were interrupted by afternoon thunderstorms—brief interludes of rain that pushed the heat away. The pilot had said that the storm front moving in from the west was different. It was expected to arrive in the late afternoon and last well into the early morning. As he walked along the road hugging the shoreline, his thoughts bent back to the heat. The air was heavy, almost cottony. He shifted his duffel bag to his other shoulder and paused to roll up his sleeves.

He stopped by the hotel on his way to Casa Tortuga. There was no one in reception, and the gift shop was closed. He walked out to the pool and found the manager having a coffee at the bar. He told Christopher the summer was the slow season, and the increase in drug violence had made the American tourists nervous about coming. There had been a kidnapping, and three bodies dumped on the highway not more than thirty miles north. Christopher asked him if the restaurant was open and he said yes. Did he want lunch? No, but maybe he would come down later for dinner. The manager mentioned that Alfonso did not know he was returning. Christopher said he had decided to come at the last minute.

As he climbed toward Casa Tortuga, Christopher stopped to take in where he was. The coast of Bermeja always staggered him. He looked out over the sea lit by a midday sun. The storm was coming. He could see it in the way the translucent blue-green waves charged and roared to shore, line after line—powerful and unrelenting. The insistency of beauty racing ahead of destruction. He remembered Helen's comments about emotions, about how emotions experienced in a place remained, so when you came back you could find them again. He had laughed at her, but maybe she was right. He missed her. But relationships were like chemistry experiments that could never be changed back into their original form.

He watched an osprey trying to catch a fish. It circled high and paused before making a headlong dive, crashing into the water and then taking off in one continuous movement. As it gained altitude, it shuddered, shaking off water. It performed the same tilted oval maneuver again. Something about the bird made him think it was young and inexperienced. He watched it repeat its maneuver one more time before it flew away hungry, disappearing east over a cluster of coconut palms.

In Bermeja word traveled fast, and as he walked to Casa Tortuga's entrance, Alfonso opened the door.

In the early evening, the wind began to pick up and the temperature dropped ten degrees. The canopies of the coconut palms began to rustle, as if gossiping about what was coming. Soon they would be bending and swaying like arms of dancers racing through the choreography of a piece they were about to perform. On the horizon, a dark line was expanding, blurring the boundary between water and air. On the west coast of Mexico, Christopher could see disturbances from far away. He watched the storm roll in. The lightning—when it came—was fierce, cracking the night sky—an outline of a mountain range, two skeletons holding hands, then three, road maps, river paths, upside-down leafless trees, the flow of blood in a body, the veins of the leaf he and Helen had felt at Willie's play. He waited to hear the thunder, to mark and measure how far away it was. He counted the seconds until the thunder came and divided by five to determine its distance. The storm was still several miles off the coast. The sea captain had taught him this calibration, and later, in school, he had learned its scientific underpinnings. Before long, the storm arrived like a cavalry of angry, hell-bent horsemen, encasing the small house in an artillery of rain.

At five P.M., Helen's flight to Manzanillo was delayed due to weather. At eight P.M. it was canceled. There was only one flight per day. The stranded passengers formed a line to rebook for the following day. Helen asked for her luggage, waited another hour to retrieve it, and at nine thirty P.M. was at the Airport Hilton. She asked the night manager if the hotel could find a driver for her. It was a twelve-hour drive, but if they left early she could be in Bermeja close to the same time as the next day's scheduled flight. And there was no certainty it would take off the following day. It was a regional airline, and she overheard a Mexican woman say, as she was waiting in line to rebook her flight, "*Ellos deciden salir cuando quieran.*" They decide to go whenever they want. Helen had traveled enough to know to look for alternative routes, plus, right now she did not like the idea of staying still for very long.

The night manager did not think he could find a driver for her by the following morning. It was late—almost ten P.M. It was too far. No one wanted to drive to Bermeja. It would be expensive. She should take the flight the following day. She asked the manager again to call a taxi or car service. He obliged but after three rings hung up. "*Ellos no están respondiendo.*"

"Could you try again?" Helen asked.

He tried one more time and held the phone out for her as if she would be able to see an answer. He let it ring twice as long, but still no answer. She asked about buses, and he said, "No, not to Bermeja, nothing direct, only to Manzanillo."

"Do you have a schedule?" He disappeared into the back office without saying why. While she was waiting for his reappearance, the bellhop came and told her his cousin would drive her. He gave her a price and she agreed.

"Six in the morning?"

"Yes, six A.M."

At five forty-five she was waiting outside the Hilton when an old once-blue truck emerged from the darkness and rolled to a stop. *This can't be the car and driver,* she thought, but it was. José Hernandez. He spoke no English, which suited her. For the past week, she had been asking questions that rarely yielded an answer she wanted, and she was tired. She said the name Bermeja to confirm that he knew where he was going. He nodded and said, "Manzanillo." The bellhop arrived and translated. He explained that José's brother lived in Manzanillo, and he would drop her off in Bermeja and then drive to his brother's house. She thought she understood the bellhop instructing his cousin to drive only on toll roads, before turning to her to add that in addition to the fare she would have to pay for gas and tolls. She agreed, and he lifted her duffel bag into the back of the truck and opened the door for her. The plastic seats were grimy and ripped in several places. She got in and rolled her window down. They were off in the cool morning air with an hour's head start on the sun.

Still on European time, Christopher awakened before dawn. As the darkness was beginning to disappear, he decided to go for a run. The storm had crossed during the night. The air was cool and clean, and as he ran down the high cliff of Casa Tortuga, he breathed in the early morning scents of coconut palms and lush vegetation he knew only by scent and color and not by name. He ran north past the long beach of Bermeja to Playa Rosa, a small beach given its name by the broken pieces of pink coral that colored its sand. It was the beginning of one of those beautiful, wild, middle-of-summer days. The high pressure following the storm had transformed the chaotic energy of the surf into clean, powerful waves that came one after another in steady, rhythmic sets. He dove into the cool water and swam out to where the waves were breaking. Flattening his torso and stretching his arms overhead, he used his hands as a plane to traverse the wave and ride it to shore. He felt as if he were dancing with an old friend. Days spent in that ocean, he reacquainted himself with its moods and movement.

An early morning mist had begun to roll in, and as he swam

out once more, he felt a riptide pulling him away from shore. He knew not to resist, and he let it take him out. He swam parallel to the shore to release himself from its hold, but he could not find its edge. The current was now taking him far outside the breakers and pulling him fast down to the cliffs. If he could get to the rocks, he could use them to anchor himself and edge around to shore. The waves were building as the tide was dropping. With so much water moving, what was risky half an hour ago was not even possible now. Body surfing back was too dangerous because he could get smashed onto the exposed reef.

He reached the base of the cliff, steadied himself, and assessed his options. The sets were coming harder now, and he would have to guard against being pounded against the rough and jagged rocks. He was about two thirds the length of a football field away from the beach. He could move shoreward with the swells, but once he was farther inside where the waves were breaking, he would have to wait for a lull and move as fast as he could around the rocks.

He anchored himself by finding grip holds in the barnacle-encrusted rocks, first bracing and then holding on so as not to get ripped off as the water sucked back. The hoped-for lulls did not come. He had to move forward in the few seconds between waves, working fast in the small space before another wave crashed onto him. He managed to move only one to two arms' lengths at a time. Half the length of a football field felt like an eternity. His hands and feet were bleeding and his arms were heavy. He had another thirty feet to go—just three or four more waves, if he could find fissures to hold himself. He saw a short lull and he scrambled fast. A massive wave doubled up without warning. He heard its roar, he looked over his shoulder, but he could not see the sky. It came down on him, slamming him hard and snatching him off the base of the cliff. He was churned and tumbled and held down. There was nothing to grasp. Like a boxer taking punches, he used his arms to protect his head. The world was spinning with no sense of up or down. Color was his only guide. He gasped for air in the white froth. He pushed and clawed and scrambled his way toward the light green glow before another dark blue wall blotted out the sun and sucked him back into the muffled turbulence.

His mind began to blink.

He could not remember how he got to shore.

For a long time after, he sat on the beach, listening to the wind and the gulls and the sound of his breathing, slowly picking the bits of rock and sea urchin needles and barnacle shards from the cuts in his side and hands.

They sped west as if racing the sun. The land was dry, and by mid-morning, her face and bare arms and the back of her neck were covered in the fine red powder of the volcanic soil. Remembering the design she had seen hennaed on the hand of a woman in Tangier, she dotted and dashed a pattern on her hand and forearm with the tip of a pencil she had in her satchel, as if recording the seagulls' cries she had heard when she and Christopher were lying on the beach in Majorca. God, if she could only go back to that time and bring the way they had been with each other forward. But they weren't playing a game, and the past could not be shaken loose. She remembered the day Nick had written his number on the inside of her wrist. She was rattled to think how easily she could have betrayed Christopher.

At some point before noon, she gave herself over to the day. She no longer felt the ridged and jagged tears in the plastic seats on the back of her legs, no longer felt the grime of the heat, or the way her long hair whipped in the wind and stuck to her face, no longer felt the hum and vibration of the truck that moved up her spine and into her teeth and then back down again.

At noon they stopped for gas and lunch thirty miles east of Guadalajara. Helen felt too hot and dirty to eat, she looked around the small shop while José ate a bowl of chicken and rice and drank a beer. She bought a bottle of water and a bandanna for her hair. As he shifted gears back onto the highway, Helen collected her handful of Spanish words and mimed her offer to drive if he got tired. He nodded but did not understand. She tried again. He thought she was urging him to go faster. "*Solo el cincuenta.*" He pointed to the speedometer—the needle wobbled just shy of fifty—and then to the floor, where his foot was pushing the pedal flat. She nodded, she understood, he was going as fast as he could. She tried again, this time offering in French. "*No entiendo.*"

Bypassing Guadalajara, they veered onto the toll road 54D. They passed through acres and acres of spiky blue agave plants. *Tequila,* she thought but did not speak aloud. She checked her phone for service but there was none. The sun was beginning to descend in front of them, and she offered José her sunglasses. Each coming hour of travel would bring him closer and closer to staring straight into the sun. He raised his hand to acknowledge her offer but shook his head.

Soon after they passed the town of Tlajomulco de Zúñiga, she began to doubt the day. Her decision would not lie flat, it kept buckling up, and now, no matter how strong her effort, it would not stay down. Was it some sense of migration that had brought her back? She didn't even know for certain where Christopher was. She replayed the conversation in her head multiple times, he had said he was going to Bermeja, but he hadn't said when. She had assumed he was on his way, he seemed to be in a hurry to get everything sorted, but he could still be in France. She could arrive and find Casa Tortuga empty.

At the rate they were traveling, she would be lucky to arrive much before nine o'clock. After she paid José and gave him a tip, she would have very little money left. And if Christopher was there, what if he were with someone? He had asked that question of her. Was that because it applied to him? She could no longer have claims on him—she was the one who had left. Christopher was practiced at looking forward and never backward. He had been so clear and formal when he called her. He was calling for an answer to a specific question, he hadn't been interested in anything else. His week-old emails, which she had read and reread, had corroborated this. She had hoped to find meaning or a message where there was none.

She fought with her mind to keep it in the present and not let it race ahead of where she was. In the course of her work at the paper, she had traveled many places to meet a man she did not know. She had never doubted her ability to handle the situation—from aging aesthetes to rugged mountain guides. And now she was being driven to the man who was still her husband, and she was nervous and anxious about what she would find and how she would act. She looked at her phone to consider calling him. Still no service. She would have to wait. The heat of the afternoon helped calm the day.

Alfonso spent the first part of the day shopping for supplies. Christopher had told him not to get much, he would take his meals at the hotel. "They could use a few more customers," Christopher said, reassuring Alfonso it was fine to leave. By midafternoon, Alfonso was off to his son's wedding in Puerto Vallarta.

At eight, Christopher walked down to the hotel and ordered the grilled fish. An attractive man and woman were having dinner together. He guessed they were both in their fifties. He overheard bits of the conversation, they spoke Swiss German. He couldn't tell how long they had been together—they seemed familiar with one another, and yet they still wanted to please each other. He had always assumed he and Helen would be like them. He left the restaurant before they did, and as he was walking up the cliff, they passed him in a jeep and asked if he wanted a lift. At any other time he would have said yes, out of curiosity to find out more about them, but he said no because he wanted to be free from any connections, from any entanglement.

Back at Casa Tortuga, he picked up his book, a biography of Alexander von Humboldt, and the cold beer Alfonso had left in the kitchen and sat down under the *palapa*.

CHAPTER FORTY-SEVEN

BERMEJA

Seventeen pages later, he heard a truck pull up, a door slam, then voices. Christopher walked to the front of the house. A young woman and a crumpled man were standing by the side of a beaten-up pickup truck.

"My God, Helen."

She turned to look at him. Both Helen and the man looked as if they had been working in fields all day.

"I thought you were in Havana."

"I was."

"What are you doing here?"

"I wanted to see you."

"How did you get here? Not in that truck?"

She nodded. "Just from Mexico City."

"That's over nine hundred kilometers. Are you mad? Do you know how dangerous that is?"

She slid her bandanna off and wiped the sweat and grime from her face. "Please don't say anything about danger to me right now."

She was too exhausted, and he was too concerned, for either one to be wary of the other.

"God, sorry, Helen." He clasped her shoulders as if to keep her from falling down. She nodded and turned to the driver, who was lifting her duffel bag from the back of the truck. She pulled money out of her jeans and counted it for him and then added a tip. She shook hands with him and thanked him.

"My flight was canceled so I had to improvise."

"Improvise?"

"There was no other way."

"No other way?"

"Why are you repeating everything I say?"

"He's not driving back tonight?" Christopher asked looking back at the truck.

"No, he has a brother who lives in Manzanillo."

"Here, give me that," he said, as she bent down to take the strap of her duffel bag. They walked inside.

"Helen, are you okay? When was the last time you slept? Can I get you anything to drink? Do you want something to eat?"

"No, thanks, just some water."

He came back with a large bottle and a glass.

He put his hand on her arm. "Are you sure you're okay?"

She nodded as she took a sip of water. "It's just all of a sudden, I feel frightened to come back here."

"Here?"

"To see you." She sank down on the sofa as if miming a water skier who had just released the rope. "I know what I did was stupid—I realized it halfway. I didn't know what was more stupid, coming to see you or driving across Mexico in a fifteen-year-old pickup truck with a man I didn't know and couldn't understand. All I could think about was if I had just waited after my flight was canceled, I would probably have understood the lunacy of coming here to see you, and I would have turned around.

"But when you called me in Havana, I realized that my trip to Cuba to research an article on John Glenroy—it wasn't him I was searching for, I was searching for you. Trying to understand his flatness, his evenness, his lack of emotion, I was trying to understand you. Find you. I thought I could find you. No matter what I said—I could never get you to react to anything. I was looking for some emotion—even if it was only anger. At times I felt I didn't exist for you, as if you couldn't see me. I wanted you to recognize me, I wanted you to acknowledge my existence—something. When I told you I was leaving, I would have given anything for you to have said, 'No, don't go,' and then I thought if I did manage to get to Bermeja, would you be here? What if you weren't? I used up all my money to pay the driver. And then if you were here, what if you were with someone—?"

"Helen, slow down. First of all, I'm very happy you're here, and I'm not with anyone."

She nodded understanding. She wanted to ask him how things were with him, but she had used all her energy and emotion to make it this far. She looked out over the dark ocean, but shut her eyes because she did not want to remember how happy she had been here with him. She needed memory to stay in its hiding place. "Seeing you after being in a pickup truck for almost sixteen hours feels disorienting. I think I really need some sleep."

"You do," he said, standing up first. "And maybe a shower. We can talk in the morning."

He picked up her duffel bag and led the way along a dimly lit path to the small house overlooking the cliff. He gave her the room next to his. He turned on the light and looked around. He checked the bathroom. "Remember to look out for scorpions," he said.

"You haven't seen any here, have you?"

"No, but just look around and check your shoes. No one has been in the house for a while." The beds were mattresses placed on solid rectangular mounds built into the floor. Helen remembered their being designed that way to ensure nothing could hide under them. Both bedrooms had windows open to the ocean.

She closed her eyes and let the hot water run down her back, trying to feel all the different rivulets of water. Her journey from Havana, filled with small curves and hooks and deflections, had felt like one of those paths. She turned and faced the hot stream of water as if to wash away all doubts and misgivings, but her conviction seemed to swirl away with the dirt and sweat of the hot journey. After she washed her hair, she said good night to him, put a towel on the pillow, and turned the light off. She stretched down deep into the cool sheets. Compared with the truck that had shaken and jolted and jarred the six hundred miles from Mexico City, the stillness of her bed felt wondrous. She listened to the sound of the waves on the rocks below. She tried to time her breathing with their push and pull as a way of slowing down her mind.

He walked back to the *palapa* and picked up his book. His back and side ached, and it hurt to breathe. He thought about what she had said. He hadn't completely followed her explanation of why she had come. She had always moved with emotion, rarely reason. She had put herself in danger driving across Mexico to see him. It was not the first time she had risked things for him—he understood that, too. He had kept facts and feelings back from her. She had filled in what she thought was missing, making assumptions, borrowing from her own life, but she was not a code breaker, and he had never tried to help her or put things back together. When she walked out, he had believed he could outrun everything, but he had come to understand that nothing protects you—neither speed nor ambition. It was not a matter of pushing ahead as fast as he could. He tried to read, but his mind kept slipping off the page. He closed his book.

Helen was awakened by the sounds of beating wings and a thud. More fast beating and a thud. Silence. She sat up and turned on the light. It flew across the room again. A small dark spot, half the size of a mango, in the corner of the room, several feet below the ceiling. She called for him. He appeared in jeans and a T-shirt. He hadn't gone to sleep yet.

"Look." She pointed high to the dark spot.

"It's a bat. It's okay, it won't hurt you. I'll get him." Christopher reached behind him and pulled his T-shirt off. A large dark bruise glittering with red claw marks curved across much of his rib cage and back.

"God, Christopher, what did you do?"

"I mistimed trying to swim back to shore."

"Mistimed?"

"I lost my footing at the base of a cliff and got crashed against the rocks by a wave."

"When?"

"This morning."

"Does it hurt?"

"A bit."

"You didn't break any ribs?"

"Don't think so."

He took his shirt in his hands and walked slowly toward the corner. He reached up and covered the bat.

"Can you open the door for me? I want to let it go at the edge of the cliffs. To minimize the chances of it flying back in."

Five minutes later he returned. "Hopefully, that's the last you will see of him."

"Hopefully?"

"You just drove across drug-cartel–infested territory in a rattletrap truck, and you're going to tell me you're afraid of one little bat?"

"Yes. And its friends and relatives, too. What are the chances it will come back?"

"Do you want to sleep in my room?"

CHAPTER FORTY-EIGHT

BERMEJA

Christopher was stretched out by the pool. As the day had brightened, it had calmed. Now all that had not been blazed away was silent and still.

"Good morning," he said when he saw her.

"I feel a lot better."

"You look a lot better."

"How is your side?"

He squinted up at the sun and looked over the water. The line of the sea wavered in the haze. He looked back at her, smiled, and eased into his answer, "Better."

"Where did you learn to catch bats?"

"Maybe Fontainebleau. Sometimes they were in the barn."

She walked to the edge of the cliff and looked down at the curve of the bay. The land was covered in coconut palms with canopies of lush greens, the beach was bleached bone white, and the water was a turquoise blue that turned a dark sapphire as it deepened. Bougainvillea covered the wall of the house with hot pink blossoms.

"God, these colors, where do they come from?"

"I remember the sea captain telling me that in World War II the cockpits of the bombers were painted green to help keep the young pilots calm. I never knew if it were true or not. I've always wanted to believe those pilots saw the same green I saw when I went exploring with the captain."

"What was his name?"

"Lee, Captain Lee. I never knew if it was his first or last name. It was always just Captain Lee."

"The Imperial War Museum would have an answer."

He looked at her, not understanding the sequence of her comments.

"About the color of the cockpits."

"Oh, right. I've never wanted to find out. What if it had been some drab color, more gray than green, and that was the last color some of those young pilots saw. Do you want some breakfast? We have some fresh mango and pineapple."

"No, thanks, maybe later. Just coffee would be great."

"We can sit over there," he said when he returned with two mugs of coffee, pointing with his chin to a small pavilion with two chaises. Next to the pavilion were two rope swings hung from a primitive-looking frame.

"Would you rather be in the sun?"

"No, this is fine."

"I don't remember those swings being there last time."

"I think the frame may have been broken. The supports look as if they've been replaced. They were here when Laure and I were little." He checked the cushions of the chaises. They were damp. He left to find two towels.

She was sitting on a swing when he returned.

"Sun," she said as a reason for moving.

He put the coffee on the ground and came and joined her. He moved slowly through the pain in his side. They sat on the swings without saying anything. She anchored her heels to the ground and moved back and forth. They both watched her shadow lengthen and shorten across the grass. She enjoyed the sense of control.

"Laure and I used to spend hours on these swings," he said after a while.

"How is Laure?"

"Fine, you knew she is having a baby?"

She nodded. "She must be due any day now. Does she know what she's having?"

"A girl."

Helen twisted her swing twice around and then let it unwind.

He watched her but did not say anything.

When she had steadied herself, she asked, "Do you think things would have been different if we had had a child?"

He bent down and snapped a blade of grass. He creased it between his thumb and index finger and split it in two. He looked at her. "I don't know." He had learned a long time ago that nothing good came from asking questions that could not be answered.

When Christopher had called her in Havana, she had wondered if his reasons were as clear as he suggested. Did it have anything to do with the two of them? But seeing him now confirmed her answer. He had always made clean decisions, as if he were making them with a knife that was so sharp it never left frayed edges. That part of him had not changed. He had mentioned the sea captain, and she remembered his telling her about him, how he would always know where he was by the color of the sea. She had lost her bearings with him. Maybe it wasn't possible to know where you were all the time. Maybe Pauling's theory of parallel lines did not apply, because knowing a person had to do with interiors, and concepts of perspective had no meaning. Or maybe there were regions where access would never be granted. She had wanted and expected too much.

She wished she had not asked him about having a child, about whether things would have been different. She knew it didn't matter—it was too late. Children pulled you under. And maybe in being pulled under, their love would have touched and flowed together and they would have become so inextricably bound that they would have believed it would have hurt too much to pull apart. But maybe that would have obscured or covered over what didn't, what hadn't, existed between them. Shouldn't they have been pulled together even if it were just the two of them? They hadn't been able to find a way for that to happen.

She wondered if the couple in Cuba had children. She had no idea how old they were—poverty obscured their age. Without children, she and Christopher were uncoupled. Their breakup had been slow, like the strand-by-strand fraying of a rope until it snapped, and they couldn't find a reason to try to mend it. They would never have a reason not to speak past one another. She had hoped they could have gotten to a place where nothing was off-limits—where she could ask him anything, and he would answer willingly. Each question and each answer would be a thread pulling them closer together. Without that there would always be a gap—parallel lines that would never cross. She couldn't pinpoint when she first noticed the gap, but she guessed it had always been there, and early on she had been so in love that she hadn't noticed. *Enamoramiento*? Was this what they had had between them in the beginning? If so, it hadn't lasted. Was that the reason there wasn't a word for it in English?

"At some point I need to make arrangements to fly home."

He braked with his feet. The abrupt movement shot daggers through his rib cage. He caught his breath, he turned to her. "Then why did you come?"

"I don't know. As I told you last night, I think I was looking for you. But I feel trampled by this place, by the memory of it. I would have given anything for you to have said, 'Don't go,' and I guess I was still trying—even after I left—to understand why you didn't. Maybe my leaving was my way of trying to get you to react to me. You couldn't love me the way I wanted to be loved. It made me feel desperate.

"I think we were probably doomed at the very start. You dissolve the boundaries of who I am. And that can be beyond wonderful, but if I feel abandoned by you, I don't have any control over the devastation. It's as if I've given up all my defenses and have nothing left to protect myself. But by coming here I realize the chance for healing can't overcome my fear of destruction. The danger for me was hoping that it could. It was a mistake—coming back here.

"I'm sorry. Maybe I had to see you one more time to be sure. When you called me in Havana, the thought of your going away for a long time—my not being able to see you—I guess it just panicked me. I've gotten through the last six months inch by inch. I'm not like you. I can't avoid looking back." Her words folded down hope.

"What do you want me to say? This is when I want to tell you to grow up, but I won't, because I don't want you to leave. Of course I would have loved to have had a child, and yes, I do think a child might have held us together, might have held us together at times in a way that we were unable to do by ourselves. You believed in us well past where you should have. Somewhere along the way I made certain I wouldn't be able to feel anything. Ambition was my way forward. I thought it could keep me safe, but all it did was keep me from feeling. Speed, velocity kept me from having to deal with anything, at least for a while."

"Why are you telling me this now?"

"When I appeared to be ignoring or resisting you, it wasn't you—I guess that's all I'm trying to say. But there's nothing I can do about any of that now. No words, no action—nothing. And do I wish I had said, 'Don't go'? I thought I had."

The cadences of his voice were full of meaning.

"If you decide to leave—I understand. I should have been better at a lot of things. No one understands that better than I do. I know I made it difficult, too difficult, for you. I get that." He looked up at her. "But I still love you."

It was no longer a question of his saying anything more.

In the late afternoon, the sun burned through a low band of clouds that sat heavy on the horizon. They walked down to the hotel so she could book her flight. The hotel manager did not understand how she could be leaving so soon, but she would give nothing up. The small plane was arranged to take her to Puerto Vallarta where she could take a flight to Dallas and then connect to a British Airways flight back to London. There was no reason for her to go back to Cuba. She had been looking for something she knew she would never be able to find. She had enough to write a small piece, something to justify her trip. Back home the summer holidays were starting. The day after Henry and Leonora's summer term ended, Louis and Henrietta were leaving for a holiday in the South of France. They had taken a farmhouse for six weeks outside of Grasse and had invited her, but she had declined the invitation. She would remind David she wanted to work through the summer months. It would be her way of making up for the almost wasted trip to Cuba.

CHAPTER FORTY-NINE

BERMEJA

He took her to dinner at the hotel. He was relieved not to see the couple who had been there the night before. They talked about her trip to Havana. She told him about the reader in the cigar factory, the beauty and the richness of the land, the bishop in Santa Clara. She told him about the gift of mangoes. She and Christopher had lived a life that was the inverse of the Cuban couple's, but she did not tell him this. They discussed her plans, they avoided themselves. He was careful to curve and weave around the debris of their marriage, like a skater skilled at making redirections seem part of a predetermined pattern.

"What are you going to do after?"

"You mean . . ."

"Yes."

"I don't know. You know I sold the firm—or what was left of it."

"I did."

"In order to sell I had to sign a noncompete for eighteen months.

Which is fine, because I don't know if I ever want to go back to all that. I can always return to practicing law. Besides I have—let's see—fifty-four more years before Tortuga's lease runs out."

"You'll get bored."

He looked around the almost empty restaurant. He looked back at her. "You're right. I will. But not for a while."

"What about the Pavesis?"

"What about them?"

"Isn't it strange or awkward to be here if they are?"

"Well, first of all, my family was here first, and second, Alfonso said Paolo went back to Milan for medical reasons. Apparently he is very ill. So I guess all the rumors about his not being able to return were false. Alfonso said Philippe has moved to Argentina. Something about polo and a ranch, but my guess is he's laying low. Said a group from Dallas came down to look at this place."

"You mean the Pavesis might sell?"

"Don't know. But I don't see Philippe managing it."

"And Marc?"

He shrugged. "I knew when I went to the authorities we would never speak again."

"There was something in the press about Marc and Ghislaine getting a divorce."

"Not surprising, really. She's a survivor—they both are. Ghislaine will marry or at least try to marry another rich man. I'd like to think Marc learned something from everything that has happened, but I'm not so sure. My guess is he'll resurface somewhere with another firm and be just as aggressive, only he'll be more careful and shrewder than before—"

"Until he isn't."

"Right, until he isn't."

"Have you seen Willie?"

"No, not since his play."

"Do you remember the line at the end about memory pulling you back and pushing you forward?"

He looked down at the palm of his right hand and ran his thumb over the ridges of cuts and scrapes. "Not sure I do."

"Christopher, I don't want the mews house. I'm not signing those papers."

"You should take it. You've always loved it."

"I loved it with you, but it's never been mine. I like my top-floor flat on Old Church Place. It suits me. It's small and cozy, and when I lock my door at night, I know I'm safe."

"No bats?"

"No bats. Just a little pigeon that sleeps on the sill of my kitchen window at the back of the building. He's always there, even on the coldest, wettest nights—all alone. And despite the filth he creates, I don't have the heart to shoo him away. I wonder if he's still there. Speaking of bats, can I stay in your room tonight?"

He nodded and glanced around the empty restaurant. "I think they want to close." They walked up the road to Casa Tortuga. Their silence was witness to their past.

In the middle of the night, she was awakened by the lights of a car going down the drive.

"Christopher, are you awake?"

"I am."

The sound of his voice told her he had never gone to sleep.

"Did you see that?"

"What?"

"The lights. A car just drove by."

"It's the guard service. They drive around at night at random hours."

"I don't remember them."

"It's just been since those drug murders occurred up the coast."

It was for her a night of impossible thoughts. Hours later she heard him get up.

"Where are you going?"

"For a walk. I can't sleep."

He closed the door behind him.

She lay in bed. She felt his absence. She felt the edges of her body. If she had been asked to draw the outline of her body when they had slept together, it would have always included his—a hand, an arm, a leg, a foot was always touching her—often his entire body if she had fallen asleep with her head on his shoulder or with his arms wrapped around her. She would never be able to take the feeling of his weight and warmth with her during the day. Edges were the ends of things, perimeters that could never be erased, where things stopped—the edge of despair, the edge of sadness, the edge of hope, of happiness, of fear. Not feeling edges was a willful act. The boundaries between them disappeared when they lay next to each other, but they always reappeared the next day. They knew who they were at night. But in the day, permission to cross was never granted.

Christopher looked up and considered the night sky. It glittered with thousands of stars. He would live and die without any consequence to the universe that he now held in his gaze. He listened for the space where the air was completely empty of all sound. But he could find none. The sounds were different at night. They were louder and closer. He listened for the curve of the waves before they exploded against the cliff, but the sound made him feel as if the world were tearing apart. He listened for what he could not see. He turned to look behind him, perhaps to accept the consequences of speed and ambition, perhaps to recognize the world he had left behind, perhaps to acknowledge the tides and gullies of his love for her. Life had emptied a place inside of him that he had not been willing to fill. He had stood guard. But he had come to understand that nothing stays still for very long.

What does it mean to love someone? Sex was the easy part. What took place that could not be seen was the difficult part. Theoretical physics has its own form of answer in the theory of entanglement. Two particles that have been close can be separated by vast distances, even light years, and still remain connected. What happens to one, happens to the other instantaneously. Entangled particles transcend space.

Christopher thought about the solitary osprey he had seen searching for sustenance the day of the storm. Humans were different. They needed each other, needed to be recognized, needed to be heard, needed to be touched, needed to share the earth and the sea and the sky to know they were alive. Helen was always trying to find metaphors to understand the world around her, forever blurring lyricism with theories of physics. She had opened her heart wide, but he had been listening from too far away.

She heard him come back when it was no longer dark.

And in the early hours of that morning, they moved with stealth past the guardians of their hearts.